FIGHTING BACK

A SCEINCE FICTION ADVENTURE STORY

BY

DAVID A EVETT

Author Note

In the book the reader should imagine himself the lead role. Imagination is the key to all inventions.

Dedication

To anyone who believed in me

Prologue

This is fiction but it could happen to you !

Table of Content

BOOK – 1
Chapter – 1

It had been a long and tiring day and I was looking forward to getting home, I'd been up since 5.30am and now it was 9.0pm. I can still remember that night, driving back from Grimsby to Doncaster. The M180 is a lonely road at the best of times, but in January, at that time of night, it is a lot worse. I'd been listening to the weather report on the radio and the forecast was "Frosty with occasional fog patches." I was driving along thinking that there was nobody but myself on the road when I saw, in the distance, twin red spots of light. My first thought was, I'm not the only mug in the world out on a god forsaken night like this! I started to speed up, playing a kind of game in my mind. I was thinking to myself, trying to guess, is it a car or a lorry, all the time I was catching him up. Id gone about a mile when WHAM! FOG! I slowed down, thinking, as soon as I'm out of this patch, I'll soon catch him up.

The fog swirled around my car, lit up by the headlamps and instead of getting thinner, the fog seemed to be getting thicker? Just as I thought that I would soon be clear, the lights, then the engine cut out, pitching me into semi-darkness! SHIT! what the hell was wrong with the bloody car now, I been having trouble with the damned thing for weeks! What a time and place to break down, right in the middle of nowhere! DOUBLE SHIT! I knocked the car out of gear and steered for the hard shoulder. Through my cursing and moaning I began to realise that something was wrong other than the engine failure. I did not seem to be mowing, the fog still swirled around the car but there was no sensation of actual movement from the car its self! I did not believe it, I was totally baffled?

My next thought frightened the life out of me! SHIT! If another vehicle was behind me, they would not see me till it was too late. I was panicking a bit as I thought about pushing the car off the motorway. I tried to open the door but it seemed to be stuck! What was happening? I tried the passenger door but that was stuck too! I turned to try the other doors, fear and panic building up all the time. All the doors and the windows were stuck fast, I couldn't open any of them! I could hear somebody shouting but didn't realise that it was me! As I was battering on the doors and windows, I caught my shin on the centre console. The pain brought me to my senses and I started to think a little bit. All four doors can't have stuck at the same time, what the hell was going on?

Suddenly all the hair on my body stood on end, just like it does when you get a charge of static electricity off a TV screen! As I looked out of the window, I could see, about six foot away, three figures. My first thought was that another car had stopped to help, after seeing I was in trouble. Relief flooded through me, then as I looked closely at my rescuers, fear started to rise again. Then I saw that they were dressed in what appeared to be diving suits and helmets; I lost my cool and started to kick and bang on the doors again. Out of the corner of my eye, I saw one of the figures raise a strange looking tube and point it at me. As I was slipping into unconsciousness one of the figures reached out and opened the door! I don't know how long I was out, but when I came round I was totally blank and disorientated. I laid still for what seemed hours, trying to remember what had happened. I raised my arm to look at my watch, I don't know why but I had to know the time. It took a few seconds of staring at my bare arm before I realised that my watch was missing! I struggled to sit up and found myself looking at a pair of bare legs; in fact, when I checked, I was completely naked! After this had slowly sunk in, I started to take notice of my surroundings. I was in a small room that had no visible doors or windows, I did, however, realise one thing, It was time to PANIC! All that kept going through my mind was, where was I, why am I here? Why was I naked? Who brought me here and what is going to happen to me?

I managed to calm down a bit and as I lay back on the slab, I tried to reassure myself by thinking, this is all a dream, I'll wake up in a moment when the alarm goes off. The slab can't have been uncomfortable because I dosed off! When I awoke, I was still a little dazed and it took me a little while to realise I was not alone. Two of the figures I remembered from the car were stood near me, as I sat up they backed away from me and started to jabber, amongst themselves or at me, I had no idea. "Look, what's going on? Why am I here? Who are you?"

I asked them, my fear growing all the time, They just stood there in their suits and helmets, I presumed, staring at me. I couldn't see their faces through the visors and this, coupled with their silence, was increasing my fear. In my rising panic, I started to shout and I was waving my arms around, I was getting more agitated by the second. "What the hell is going on? Who are you? Answer me, for Gods sake! I got an answer of sorts from the figure nearest to me, he reached out with the tube thing he was carrying and touched me on my left arm. My whole arm went numb! That did it, I really panicked then! I leapt off the slab and started running about like a mad man! One of the figures tried to grab me , but I pushed him away and as the other one stated to raise his tube weapon I hit him. I hit him right in the face, the result so surprised me, I stopped dead. When I'd hit him, his helmet flew off and he shot back and hit the wall with a thwack. He slid down till he was sat on the floor but it was his face that shocked me! It was as white as snow, his eyes were a really dark blue and I couldn't see any ears, just slits! I just stood there, I was so stunned I couldn't move! My mind was in turmoil. ALIENS! Couldn't be, can't be. BLOODY HELL! ALIENS! Time to panic. Again!

Before I could get started the other alien "shot me with his tube, down I went into a deep sleep. When I came around again, I was on the slab, only this time I was wearing something, Handcuffs! My hands were tied fast behind me, my left arm was starting to thaw out and I was in agony with pins and needles.There must have been some sort of observation window, because I'd only been awake a few minuets when part of the wall slid back and four of the aliens came into the room. They all stood well back this time and one of them kept gesturing me to follow them. I swung my legs off of the slab and sat up, I went that dizzy that I nearly passed out again! I shook my head and the dizziness started to clear, I stood up and staggered towards one of the aliens, he jumped back and raised his tube. He didn't have to fire because by this time I was on the floor being sick!

One of the aliens started to kick me and he was jabbering away. presumably telling me to get up. I struggled to my knees, I waited a bit, I had to let the room stop spinning, then somehow, I got to my feet. The one who must have been in charge motioned for me to follow him and he set off, with me staggering behind. The others followed behind me as we went along a corridor, I don't know how long it took, as I was still in a daze. We passed other doors and I wondered who or what was behind them. We finally stopped outside a door, the leader did something, I don't know what, and tho door opened. Time to panic again! The view I had as the door opened was like looking into an operating theatre. All the stories I had read and the films I seen soon came back to me of aliens cutting up specimens. Before I could really get going, they cut the legs out from under me then lifted me onto the table. The only thing I could do was to shout and curse them. This I did quite a bit of. I laid there like a pound of mince while two of the aliens stuck probes and wires in all sorts of funny places, and while I'm thinking ,why me, dear God, why me? One of the aliens gave me an injection and I thought, at least I wont feel it when they start cutting. I laid there waiting but, I wasn't feeling tired and as they worked around me I had the horrible thought that they would cut me up while I was a still awake. I'm not a religious man but I" prayed then and I prayed hard. After awhile they removed the wires and probes. When this was done, one of the aliens put a box like instrument around his neck, turned it on and spoke to me!

At first I was gob smacked! I could understand him! He had to repeat himself as I missed what he'd said the first time.
"You will not be harmed if you do not resist"
Before I had a chance to reply, he turned off the box and started to twitter to the others. By this time my legs had started to thaw out and I was moving them to restore the circulation. As the aliens saw me doing this they rushed to strap me down. As my fear returned, I started to struggle more. They had got my arms strapped but not my legs, one of them tried to grab my legs but I managed to kick him. He went backwards, down and moaning, in a heap, the others backed away, not keen to tackle my thrashing legs. The guards and the"doctor started twittering fit to bust, I could tell from the gestures that they were discussing me. The doctor had the last twit then put the box on and spoke to me.

"Do not be afraid" Easy for him to say, he wasn't where I was.

"No harm will come to you, I only wish to take skin and body fluid samples. We do this with all our specimens. "

Cheeky sod, I thought, specimen indeed.!

"What happens after the samples are taken? " I asked. I was dreading the answer but I had to know.

"You will be returned to your compartment. "

Before I could ask anymore questions, he turned oft the box and the guards started to twitter again. An Argument seemed to be going on accompanied by a lot of arm waving, nobody seemed to be winning. All of a sudden the door swished open and the noise stopped Judging by the guards stances, someone of importance had just walked in. When he had stopped twittering to the doctor and guards he held his hand out and took the box from the doctor. He was the first alien I'd got a really good look at. The doctor had on a mask and the one I'd hit had been seen in a haze. I didn't remember much about it. He was about five foot tall, slim and really, really ugly, by earth standards and he was bald! He switched on the box and spoke to me.

"You have caused a great deal of trouble, you have killed one of my crew and injured another. If there is any more trouble from you, you will be drugged till we reach our home world. Do you understand?"

I nodded my head and in a croaky voice said.

"Yes"

"Good"

Then he paused before speaking again, as though he was speaking to a child.

"We will be travelling for many light years, stopping at other planets to gather other exhibits for our zoo "

With that he handed the box back to the doctor and with final twit he left. After he had gone, the guards and the doctor relaxed and began twittering to each other. I lay very still while the doctor finished taking the samples he wanted.

"What does he mean when he said a zoo?"

The doctor looked at me, turned to put the box on, then asked me to repeat what 1'd said. When I had done so, he replied.

"You will be put on show in our interplanetary zoo with the female of your species. "

Oh boy, this was too much!

"There you will breed and your young, when of a suitable age, will sent to other zoo's."

After pausing he continued to explain what would happen to me.

"You will be in our zoo for a very long time, the injection I gave you is a longevity drug. You will not die unless you have an accident ,nor will you grow old. "

This was great news, to live forever in an alien zoo! I asked some more questions.

"So your race lives forever does it? Won't your planet become overpopulated, and when it does, what then?"

"We have colonised the worlds closest to us and our conquest carries on. There will be no shortage of planets or slaves either. " he said.

"What happens when you meet a race of beings that will fight back?" I asked.

"We have had two set backs with alien cultures, one in particular has cost us a great deal in spacecraft and crews."

"Who are they?"

"They are called XIOBARGS, a very war like race. They are almost suicidal in their attacks on our ships and will go anywhere to fight us. They are fearful creatures. "

Great stuff! Not only am I to become a zoo exhibit, there's a chance a suicidal, homicidal race of aliens might blow this ship up!

I wanted to ask more questions but the doctor turned the box off and carried on poking and prodding. After about ten minutes he spoke to the guards, they came over and motioned for me to follow them. They gave me a pair of trousers to put on and then we left the room. As we walked back down the corridor, I wondered which door my "mate" was behind. As we passed a door, about three up from my cell, there was such a screech. The next second the door opened and out rushed a guard. He was the one doing the screaming, right behind him came something you only see in nightmares!

The guard charged straight into our group, knocking two of my guards onto the floor. He recovered his balance and ran, screaming down the corridor, the nightmare stopped when it came up against the two guards still standing. What happened next still makes me sick to think about it. "IT" grabbed the nearest guard and ripped his head clean off his shoulders! Pausing only long enough to discard the headless body, it attacked the next one. The guard didn't have a chance to fire his tube weapon because the creature tore his arm off. The other two guards had by this time, gotten to their feet, one started to run, the other tried to get his weapon into action. The creature ripped his throat out! It then picked up a tube and fired at the running guard but missed.

The speed of this thing was incredible! It then turned to look at me. My mind had gone numb while all the action had taken place and was only just starting to work. It was only slightly taller than me but it was built like a brick shithouse! It's face can only be described as all teeth with two eyes above, Its skin was a deep crimson and its claws were really long and dangerous looking. We stood and stared at each other for what seemed like ages to me. Picture it, I'm stood there, with my hands tied behind me and just in front of me is psychopathic nightmare! I thought to myself, I won't even get to see what my mate looks like, knowing my luck, she probably looks worst than this thing!

My brain was screaming RUN to my legs, but it was my bowels that had instead! Suddenly, it turned it's attention in the direction the guard had run, with a growl at me, it ran in the opposite way. I slumped to the floor, shaking all over with fear and relief. As I looked to my left, I could see some of the guards coming towards me. They had different weapons than the tubes and they held them at the ready. When they got to me they stopped and surveyed the carnage. They left one guard with me, he looked very relieved indeed, the rest followed the creature. The way they acted, I didn't think that they wanted to catch up with it! From further down the corridor came the sounds of conflict. A few screams, a hideous howl and then silence. After a few minutes the other guards came back and this time there was an air of confidence about them. It was obvious that the creature was either dead or at least under control. I was still a bit shaky as the guards helped me up but instead of taking me to my cell, they escorted me back to the doctors room. As we proceeded down the corridor, I could see burn marks on the walls and a lot of white stuff. This turned out to be the blood of my captors, I don't remember seeing any when the creature attacked my guards. The shock must have blanked out my memory. As the guards ushered me into the doctors lab they removed the handcuffs and as I stood there rubbing my wrists, the doctor put on the box and spoke. " I am going to examine you, the Xiobarg didn't attack you, did it?" So thats what the Xiobargs look like. No wonder these guys were frightened of them! I replied to the doctors question.

"No it didn't attack me although I could do with a change of trousers and a bath."

"You were very lucky, they usually attack anything and everything. "

"It must have heard the guards returning, what are the burn marks on the walls caused by?" I asked.

"The guards had to use blasters on it. Its a pity they had to kill it because it was the first Xiobarg we have ever had alive. It would have made a wonderful exhibit as it would have been the only one in captivity."

When I thought about it, I could now feel sorry for all those animals kept in zoos around the world and were deprived of their freedom just so humans could gawp at them. Now I was in that same position and it didn't feel good. I asked the doctor if I was to be fed and watered and he told me that food and a change of clothes would be waiting for me in my cell. Before I left I asked him what his home planet was like. "It is not much different from your own planet or any of the others we have called at. The only major differences are the colour of our sun's and the gravity of our world is only a third of yours." "What about the Xiobarg world, " I asked

"That thing seemed a lot stronger than your guys, it threw them around like so much dead grass " I said.   "Their planets gravity is about five times greater than ours so when we brought it onto our ship, which is geared to our gravity, its speed and strength increased to five times our own. Yours would be about three times greater." He replied.

There was no wonder that I'd killed that guard! I asked some more questions.

"How far are we from my world? "

He did some thing to a machine behind him, then turned to me.

"We are about three hundred light years away and at the moment we are approaching a planet we have located to see if we can pick up any more specimens, "

JESUS. H. CHRIST Three hundred light years! I tried to work out the distance in miles, light travels at 186,000 miles an hour. Multiply this by 3, then add a couple of zeros and you have 558000001 BLOODY HELL! I wished I hadn't asked now, I was more depressed than ever! I had no idea where we were or where we'd been The only thing I was sure of was that with every second I was getting further from the Earth. It was with a feeling of utter despair and loneliness that I was led back to my cell. Well, that was that, even if I managed, by some stroke of luck, to hijack a spaceship, I still wouldn't know which way to go to get back to Earth. I looked around my cell, realising this was to be my "hone' for awhile, then I noticed a couple of dishes on a table. After I washed and changed I started on the food. There were vegetables and what looked like meat, it was a bit tough but beggers can't be choosers, so I started to eat. As I was eating I thought this meats a funny colour, not like the beef on Earth. This meat was a deep red, like crimson? Suddenly I started to gip! It's the bloody XIOBARG! I flung the dish away from me and I was sick all over the place. It was some tine before I stopped gagging. The door slid open and in came a couple of guards and the doctor.

"What is the matter, are you ill?" he asked me.

"You bastards, you expect me to eat that, that creature?"

Before I could say anything else he raised his hand and spoke.

"To us the Xiobarg is a lower form of life, and so is every other animal or species we encounter. Did you not eat meat on your planet?"

"Well yes," but he stopped me from speaking by raising his hand.

"All you have done is eat the flesh of a lower order of animal, there is nothing wrong with that."

"I know" he stopped me again.

"It does not matter where it came from, all other creatures are lower than us and as such are ours to do with as we please!"

"Do you mean that if I died you would eat me too?" I asked

"As long as you were not diseased, yes. " He replied.

Well, theres a smack in the eye for the human race. To be thought of as nothing but food by a bunch of pasty faced half assed aliens! I asked him who the hell they thought they were!

"We are the UXTOMALS, nothing will or can stop our domination of space." He said.

"Why haven't you attacked my planet then?" I asked.

"Your planet has only just been discovered as it is thousands of light years from my own. When we have destroyed the

Xiobargs and the Numals then we will spread out this way in conquest, nothing will stop us. The information in our data banks will enable us to conquer thirty new worlds, yours included. Now do you require more food?" He sounded really smug.

"Not at the moment, thank you I couldn't face anymore Xiobarg just yet." Sarcasm was lost on him.

With that he turned out of the door and left me to think about what he had said. I tried to convince myself that the human race would stop them, but the more I thought about it, the more depressed I became.

If they had larger weapons like the ones I'd already seen, then the Earth had nothing to stop them.

What could I do? If this ship reached their home planet the location of the Earth and the other planets would give their spaceships the go ahead to attack at any time they chose! I tried to think of ways to stop this ship but I'd need an army! I had know way of knowing how big this ship was, it could contain a hundred Uxtomals or a thousand. I didn't know where the controls were, how they worked or anything! With these happy thoughts going round in my head I laid down and drifted off to sleep. I was having the most vivid dream, I could hear screams and shouting, there were lights flashing and alarms going off all over the place. Suddenly, the ship tilted and I fell of my slab! The pain of hitting the floor made me realise that I wasn't dreaming! The ship was under attack! Whoever was attacking had presented me with a opening and closing door and the bottom half of a guard. I waited for it to fully open, then jumped into the corridor. Just in front of me was the top half of the guard When the ship was attacked he must have fallen into the open door way and the door had closed, cutting him in half! Luckily for me his gun was in the corridor. As I stood there trying to figure out how the gun worked, three guards came running towards me. This is it, I thought, its either me or them. They kept on coming and to my surprise ran straight by me! It wasn't long before I found out why! Charging after them was about ten tons of hair, horns and teeth! I jumped through the door with the dead guard in it. I found a table and as the door closed I jammed it up against it. The monster couldn't have seen me as it charged straight by, still after the guards. After about five minutes, I removed the table but the door stayed shut! Great stuff, I'd locked myself in another cell but this time with half a guard as company! I suddenly remembered the gun, I picked it up from here I'd dropped it while wedging the door. I began to examine it and to my delight I found a trigger mechanism. I pointed the gun at the door and pulled the trigger. I expected something to happen but not the result I did get! The whole door was blasted off and the back flash singed a lot of hair off as well I looked at the gun then at the door, WOW! Next time I fire it, I'll stand a bit further back! I stepped cautiously, into the corridor and began slowly to walk towards the doctors room. Some of the other doors to the other rooms were open and I cautiously looked in them. Most were empty but one of them had what looked like an Earth woman in it. She didn't move as I walked over to her and I was worried she might be dead. As I leaned over her I could see she was still breathing but only just. I went back into the corridor, I had to find the doctor fast, and before I set of I wanted to mark the door in some way so I would know it and I saw a dial on the side of the gun and after turning it I was rewarded with a low power energy bean. I burnt a large circle on the wall and then continued down the corridor in search of the doctor. As I advanced I came across another dead guard and I stripped him of his belt and tube weapon. When I got to the doctor's room, the door was open and when I looked into the room I saw the doctor sat on the table with his head in his hands. As I got closer I could see he had a deep gash on his head that was oozing white blood. He looked up at me with a blank stare, then with a start, he recognised me. When he saw the gun in my hand it made him relax just as quickly. I searched around till I found the box and hoping it still worked I put it on.

"What happened to the ship, who attacked it?" I asked

For some moments he just stared at me, then he spoke.

"I don't know, when we were first attacked I was knocked out"

"How do we find out what happened?" I asked.

As I talked I began looking for a bandage or something to put on his head. He must have realised what I was doing because he pointed to an upturned cabinet. I kept my eye on him while I searched and soon returned to his side with the bandages. As 1 wrapped his head, I told him I wanted him to come with me and look at the earth girl. After helping him up he turned to a computer terminal and pressed a few buttons. He read the screen, and I watched his face, If anything he went even paler, I asked him what was wrong. He said.

"According to this, all the control deck and living quarters have been totally destroyed! That means 98% of the crew will have been killed!" He continued" There won't be anybody alive, up there." Somebody will be alive, surely there will be injured?" He seemed to forget I was new to this space ship lark.

"No one could have survived according to this, it is all open to space If anyone did survive the initial strike, they would have been blown into space! " He said. As the real impact of this news hit him, he just seemed to shrink! I caught him and lifted him onto the table. I asked if there was any other medicines I could get him, he pointed to a small box near the computer and when I opened it, it contained a syringe and phials. I passed it to him then helped him sit up. He filled the syringe and injected himself. I laid him back down and after about a quarter of an hour he looked and sounded a lot better. While he had been recovering, I had been packing a bag with bandages and I also shoved the syringe and phial of medicine into It. As we moved into the corridor I asked him why the rest of the ship had not blown into space, "Automatic airlock doors would have come into operation at the first breach of the outer shell. " he said.

"So it is still possible some of the crew might be alive, but trapped between airlocks?" I said, more trying to cheer him up than anything else. " At that time the maximum of crew would be away from their quarters, you see it was the main meal time." So that was that, they'd all been getting stuck into Xiobarg pie & chips when WHAM! Goodnight Vienna! I asked him where we were in relation to the crews quarters and found out we were in the lowest part of the ship. By this time we had come to the door that I had marked. As we stepped through into the cell I bumped into the doctor who had stopped dead in his tracks. There in front of us, leaning over the girl, was what I can only describe as a large cat. As he looked up, I grabbed for my gun, but before I could pull it from it's holster he spoke.

"Do not touch the gun or my mate will kill you"

I looked round and there to the side was another one. This one had a gun trained on me. I relaxed slightly and asked him.

"What are you doing with the girl?"

I was seeing if I could help her Earthman. "

EARTHMAN! " How did you know I was an Earthman?" I asked in surprise.

"My Own race has been travelling in space for centuries and we have visited many planets. Unlike the Uxtomals, we were peaceful visitors. We would have contacted you before long. as we did several worlds with intelligent life forms "

I was astounded! this is probably were all those U. F O sightings came from. Then I thought of what he'd said and asked.

"What did you mean, were a peaceful visitor?"

He took a deep breath before he replied.

"When the Uxtomals discovered our planet, we were overjoyed. Here we thought, at last, is another race capable of space travel. We hoped that they would help us all advance into the future together. All they did , though, was to kill and enslave my people. Those they didn't kill they put to work , building advanced bases for their space fleets. We had only spoken to them, we newer set eyes on an Uxtomal till they had destroyed our cities and towns. "

Suddenly the girl moaned and snapping myself out of my thoughts, I urged the doctor over to her side. After a quick examination, the doctor said we had better take her back to his work station where he would be better equipped to deal with her injuries. He gave her a pain killing injection before the Catman and I carried her back to the surgery. While all this had been going on, the Catwoman had not taken her eyes, nor her gun, off of the doctor. I could see the hate in her eyes and I was afraid she might kill him before he could fix up the girl.

While we carried the girl, I asked the catman what his people called themselves.

"Our planet was known as TAREX. My own name is Dundal and she is Septan."

He then asked me my name, to which I replied, David. I told him I didn't know the girl's name. The doctor, meanwhile, had been working on the girl. I asked him how she was.

"Bad" He replied, "very bad. She has internal injuries and several broken bones. I don't think she will live."

GREAT! The only human within millions, possibly billions of miles and she would probably die! The doctor turned to me as though he had been reading my mind and said.

"I'm sorry, I'll do what I can but, I think It's hopeless"

Two days later, the Earth girl died. She newer opened her eyes. I felt a really deep sense of loss, It was silly really as I'd never got to know her. It was probably because she was from Earth. While we had watched the girl, we had taken turns to roam around. Dundal and I had searched as much of the ship as we could. We'd located the hangers with the smaller scout ships in. I only knew this because of Dundal. Apparently these were the ones used to visit the planets. There was also a lot of cages, which, thankfully, most of were empty. We searched around and to my joy, we found a dog! It was a scruffy looking mongrel but I fell in love with it straight away.

It turned out to be a bitch and at first she was a bit scared of Dundal. It must have been awesome looking up at a six foot cat! Within the two days we had scoured the ship, we failed to find anybody else alive. After the girl died we blew the doorway into the control deck. We'd found some of the Uxtomal suits and, after modifying them, had put them on first. Hardly any of the computers were damaged but the crew were all dead. With the positions of the bodies, it looked like the blast had killed them. As no one could work or read the computers Dundal suggested we go back for the doctor. We were shattered when we got back so we decided to go back to the control deck the next day. All four of us returned to the control deck. The doctor could operate some of the computers but not all, he told us the ship was useless but that some of the smaller scout ships had managed to escape the ship Dundal suggested we do the same. We packed everything we could into a thirty man scout ship and prepared to leave. The doctor was in charge as nobody else could understand the Uxtomal writing. When he pressed the button for the hanger doors to open, nothing happened! When he'd told us what was wrong, Septan wouldn't believe him. She said it was some sort of trick and was all for killing him there and then. I started to argue with her and she accused me of being in league with him! The situation was getting rather heated when Dundal shouted making us all stop.

"Shut up all of you. Septan stop being so stupid and think. It's obvious the release mechanism is damaged due to the attack. The only thing to do is to blast our way out. We will be stuck together for who knows how long so lets try and work together, shall we. "

He then turned towards the doctor and said.

"Which console works the forward blasters?

After the doc had pointed out the blaster controls we looked at each other and realised how foolish we'd been. I only wished

I'd thought of what Dundal had said, After about five minutes and three tries Dundal blew out the hanger bay doors. The doc started up the engines and we set off into the unknown. Dundal urged the doc to get us up to maximum speed as soon as possible. When I asked why he turned to me with a look that said, I'm glad we didn't contact your planet if there all as thick as you. But instead he said.

Whoever attacked the Uxtomal ship may still be around and with the tire power they obviously have, we wouldn't last five of your Earth minutes. Now do you understand?"

I felt even more stupid than I had after the argument! I asked if there was anything I could do and received a curt no from Dundal. I sat at the back of the control room feeling like à spare wick at a candle makers wedding! Next thing, Dundal sat up straighter in his chair and started fiddling with and turning dials. I asked it anything was wrong with the ship. We were all wearing a communicator box so what ever was said was translated into the others language. They all looked at me as if I'd just appeared out of nowhere! I got a sneer from Septan, a blank look from the doc and a indulgent one from Dundal. He said.

"I keep forgetting that you know nothing of space craft. Well, my Earth friend, we are being followed by three fighters." "Are they the ones that attacked the Uxtomal ship?" I said, feeling more stupid than before.

"Yes, they are Xiobarg fighters." Dundalk said. The doc was absolutely terrified! " Can we out run then?"I asked.

Dundal replied and it wasn't the answer I wanted but it was the one I expected.

"No, we will have to fight them. Fortunately, we have the fire power and our screens will be able, to absorb their energy beams. But if they hold us up long enough for the mother ship to get into range, we've had it."

Well there it was, if the big ship hit us there wouldn't be diddly squat left. I asked Dundal if there was anything I could do, should I man a gun, throw bricks, spit or what. He said the defences were controlled by the computers so I could just sit back and relax. RELAX! I couldn't relax till I'd been to the toilet! I thought, if this keeps up I'm going to run out of clean trousers! The ship suddenly lurched and before I could ask what had happened Septan said. "The've opened fire, that was the shields deflecting the fighters beams. If more beams hit us in rapid succession, it will short out the shields." Then our ship lurched again.

Why don't we fire back?" I asked, My voice was starting to rise a little.

" We have." Septan was sitting very calmly, as though she was on pleasure cruise! I think what was getting to me the most was the fact that I couldn't see anything. I asked Dundal if there was anyway we could watch what was going on. He asked if I was sure that was what I wanted , then when I nodded I did, he pressed some buttons and a large screen in front of us suddenly showed the rear of the ship. I was watching, fascinated and I was counting the enemy fighters. I was a bit dismayed to see there were four of them. When I mentioned this to Dundal he told me there'd been six a minute ago! When I asked what had happened to the others, I got one of those patronising looks. Apparently the ships defences had knocked out two of them and the only thing left was a couple of fading lights on our screen.

I looked at the radar seen just below the viewing one and asked Dundal what the big blip was. He told me it was the Uxtomal mother ship. He then turned to talk to the doc about increasing our speed. I was still watching the radar screen and I must have made some sort of sound because Dundal asked me what the matter was now. I could only point to the screen. On it had just appeared what could only have been the Xiobarg mother ship. Dundal turned up the veiwing screen to full power, and there it was. It was impossible to guess it's actual size, it was a real mother! I looked at Dundal and he looked at me. I didn't get the chance to ask any questions because he answered them all straight away.

"If we can knock out these remaining fighters, there is a slim chance we can out run the Xiobarg ship. We have to got rid of the fighters first because most of our power is going into the shields Without the screens on we can make five times more speed."

"If we cut the power inside the ship to a minimum, would that make any difference to our speed?" I asked.

Dundal smiled at me and said, "There's hope for you yet Earthman." He began pressing switches and turning dials. I glanced at the doc and he was doing the same, his hands flying around like bees wings. What astounded me about the doc, though, was tho look of sheer terror on his face! I nudged Dundal and pointed to the doc. He must have read my mind because he asked Septan if she thought she could take over the doc's controls. Without a moments hesitation she said. " I have been watching the Uxtomal and know enough now to fly the ship."

Dundal looked at me and nodded at the doc, then motioned to the back of the control room. I gathered he wanted me to remove the doc and keep watch over him. At least it was something to do. When I asked the doc to move and let Septan take over, he just gave me a blank look. The injury, then the thought of the Xiobargs chasing him had sent him into a blue funk! I asked him again to move but he just ignored me. I got a hold of his arm, and he jerked out of my grip, he started to mutter.

"Must get away, they mustn't get me, they are animals, inferior, I'm. "

That's when I hit him. He went out like a light! I'd motioned to Septan what I was going to do, she took over straight away. I carried the doc over to one of the chairs at the back and strapped him in. Suddenly the ship gave a tremendous lurch, being the only one not strapped in, I was flung about the control room. I wasn't seriously hurt but my left arm, back and my legs were covered in bruises.

What happened?" I groaned.

" The mother ship just fired. It's a good job she's at extreme range or we would be finished. " replied Septan.

Dundal gave us cause for concern when he informed us that our defence screen was only operating at 70% because of the energy released by the hit. I asked if we could shoot back but was told by Dundal that we were out of range for our guns. Then he said. "There's only one fighter left now, the Xiobarg ship fired two beams but one of their fighters got in the way, luckily for us. If both shots had hit us we would have been defenceless as our screen would have been overloaded and broken down completely."

Within the next five minutes we had two pieces of luck. Our guns crippled the last fighter and as it spun out of control, the mother ship fired but hit it instead! Dundal didn't wait, he put all our power into the engines and with every second the Xiobarg ship became a smaller speck on our radar screen. We all relaxed. I checked the doc, he was still out. Dundal and Septan started the automatic repair system and as there didn't seem to be anything to do, I suggested we get something to eat. It took us a few minutes to get the galley going and I avoided anything that looked like meat! Septan informed us that she had put the ship on auto pilot so we weren't needed in the control room. Dundal and I carried the doc into a cabin and laid him on a bunk. He was still out, wether from my hitting him or from nervous exhaustion, I don't know. We slept our way through three days. We didn't know where we were or where we ware going, this was mainly because we didn't know where we had started from! On the forth day, a loud blaring sound startled me from my sleep. I groped my way forward to the control room. Over the last three days, we had combed the ship inside out and knew every inch of it. The doc had recovered quickly when he found out we had got away from the Xiobarg ship. When I got to the control room, everybody else was there. Dundal checked the computer and to our immense relief found it was a planet we were coming up to. For a minute I'd thought the Xiobargs had found us! I could tell from the look on the doc's face that he'd thought the same! Dundal put it up on the view screen and we watched it getting larger the nearer we got. The doc thought he recognised it as one of the worlds that the Uxtomals had visited for specimens. Before any of us could ask questions he said if it was the planet he was thinking of it was uninhabited by any intelligent life forms. He added that it could, however, support our kind of life. I suggested we land and check the outside of the ship for damage. Everyone agreed to this suggestion. It seemed to take ages to make planet fall. I was beginning to get the hang of this space talk! We cruised around till we found a suitable spot to land. Once on the ground we relaxed and began making plans to explore this new world. I asked the doe what the Uxtomals had found here.

"Just animals, we collected a few of them for specimens. We found the water and plants drinkable and edible too." He said.

This was great news! We would be able to top up our water tanks even though, with the recycling plant, we would have enough for years. We had " tons of food, all concentrated, but, fresh is best. We put our sidearms on and collected a few bags for what ever plants we found. Dundal lifted the hatch and lowered the ramp and we trooped outside. I called the dog(I still hadn't given her a name) to me, and we set off. Every time the dog went near the doc, all her hair stood up and she growled. I think the doe suspected that she didn't like him! It felt good to stand on solid ground again, even if it wasn't my own world. My own world! Would I ever see it again! Barring accidents, I'd got forever to find it. We had gone about two miles when out of some trees, charging towards us, came a flesh and bone tank! It was like the one on the ship that 1'd seen after we were attacked but about five times bigger! The dog had disappeared and I tried to emulate her! I ran as fast as I could straight towards a clump of trees, I didn't stop till I reached them! The creature had the body of an elephant but it's head was more like a crocodiles with horns! It was standing where we had been only moments before. I could see the doc but not Dundal or Septan. While I wondered what to do, an energy beam hit the creature just behind it's ear. It just shook it's head and turned towards where the shot had come from. Either the beam was too low powered to kill it or this was one tough cookie! I pulled my own gun and turned the power level up to full. Before I could fire another beam hit it right between the eyes. It collapsed in a heap. When I saw Dundal and Septan approaching it, I came out of my cover and walked towards them. We all met up about ten yards from the beast. I suddenly remembered the dog, I called and whistled but she didn't come. Well, I thought, that's another link with my world gone. I was starting to feel sorry for myself when, with a shudder, the beast started to get up! We couldn't believe it! To say we came from different planets, we all had the same idea! We ran as fast as we could back to the ship and didn't stop till the ramp was up! After we had taken off, I found out where the dog has gotten too. We'd left the ramp down and she had run back aboard! I now had a name for her. Hero! I told the others and the name raised a laugh. I thought it was laughter, it sounded weird, I didn't think my laugh sounded weird to them, after all they were the aliens, not me! The doc informed us that when they had explored the planet the first time, they'd lost a couple of crewmen to a similar animal. When I asked him why he hadn't told us this before he said he'd forgotten! BRILLIENT! We were swanning around an alien planet like it's our own back yard. It's full of creatures that if they don't bite, claw or sting you will spit in your eye, and he's forgotten to tell us!

"That beast looked a lot like the one you had on your ship, only bigger?" I said.

"Yes, " he replied "that was an infant"

How did you get it away from the adult?" I asked.

"We shot the adults with the energy rifles and then tranquilised the young one. "

I asked him if there was any rifles on board this ship and he told us they should be in lockers near to the ramp. I couldn't believe it!

He'd put all our lives at risk by letting us walk around with pistols. To say I was annoyed was putting it mildly. I called him a few names. He wanted to know what a bungalow head was! Muttering , dumb shit, under my breath, I went to get a drink, I resolved to load up with enough weapons to wipe out an army, next time, before I set foot outside the ship again! I asked if anybody had looked at the outside of the ship for damage but nobody had so we didn't know if there was any damage or not. I asked the doc if there was any more planets close to our position but he didn't know. If there was any damage it would have to wait.

There was nothing else to do so I started asking questions about the ship and how to control it. After so long they got fed up with me so I asked the doc who or what the Numals were.

He replied

"They are a race similar to the Uxtonals except they're a green colour and only fight in self defence. They are the race that gave us the knowledge to build spacecraft. They only occupy one world out on the rim of our galaxy. Soon we will have conquered them completely and they will be our slaves."

"Some friends you turned out to be, biting the hand that fed you, How did the Xiobargs get into the picture," I said it in a sarcastic tone but the communicator box cut out the voice inflection.

"We met them well beyond our galaxy, they were on a conquest of their own. We tried to communicate with them, as they were as strong in technology as we were. But they just started blasting. We had no choice but to fight". He made it sound as though the Uxtomals were little angels.!

I said.

"I see, you only attack races that are weaker than you are and if they are as strong or stronger you want to make peace. It sounds to me that you are a race of bullies"

"Did not the people on your planet make war with each other"

"Yes, but"

"Was not the one who started the war stronger than than the other?

"Yes, but"!

"I think you are a hypocrit to suggest the Uxtomals are the only ones to do this."

Well what could I say to that! Not a lot really! So I told him what he could do with his people and where to shove them, Then I went to get something to eat.

Chapter – 2

Well we swanned around in our space ship for four months. In all that time we'd visited different planets, all occupied by dangerous plants and even more dangerous animals. I'd lost Hero on one trip. She charged after a weird looking lizard into some bushes and all I heard was an horrendous wail and then nothing. I'd tried to peer through the bushes and had even walked around them, there was no sign of her! I'd just started to walk forward with the intention of searching the bushes when Septan stopped me. She'd shot one of the lizard things and she threw it into the bushes. There was that wail again then silence! I said" "There must be some sort of animal in there" and got my blast rifle ready to fire incase it charged. Septan got hold of my arm and gently told me that the bushes were the animal! Well I couldn't believe it! "They look like ordinary bushes to me" I said.

"Yes" she said "The outer ring of branches was only camoflage just to lure prey inside in search of food and shelter". She said she was sorry but it had probably eaten both the lizard and Hero. I was shattered, I'd gotten really fond of Hero. Then I started to get mad. It wasn't fair, first the girl and now the dog. It might not bring Hero back but it sure relived the build up of emotion. I raised my rifle and blasted the bush to bits. It wailed and wailed so much Dundal and the doc came running up thinking we were being attacked by a horde of monsters.

When we told them what had happened, Dundal had a go at the bush as well. All we left was a hole in the ground.

The next planet we landed on a few weeks after I'd lost Hero seemed totally deserted of any kind of animal life. We had landed in a large clearing and just lounged about for a few days. One night the doc decided to go for a walk around the clearing. As we hadn't seen anything dangerous, he went alone. When he didn't come back the next morning, we went to look for him. We found his remains after about half an hour of looking. His remains consisted of his blast rifle, pistol and belt buckle plus various other metal objects such as buttons, these were a bit corroded. I don't think we would have realised what had happened to him if Septan hadn't stepped under the tree to fetch the metal bits. Something dropped onto her arm and she screamed so loudly that it stopped us dead in our tracks. Dundal was the first to recover and he dragged her back into the clearing. He was just in time, hundreds of the things fell just where she had been standing. They looked just like woodlice only bigger!

Dundal grabbed the thing of her arm and he let out a howl and jumped back, his hand was badly burned! Septan must have passed out with the pain, I pulled out my pistol and put it on the lowest setting and shot the thing off of Septans arm. There was a hole right through her arm! Dundal was pouring water from his bottle on to his hand. Seeing him do this, I did the same with Septans arm. When 1'd finished putting a bandage on both of them, I got a stick and started prodding the thing about, It was quite dead and then to my amazement the end of the stick melted right there in front of my eyes. It had the same effect as acid has on flesh and bone! If hundreds of them had fallen on the doc, there was no wonder we'd only found the metal bits. They would take longer to dissolve.They'd dissolved him and his clothes in seconds, he wouldn't have stood a chance and he wouldn't have been able to shout! Dundal and myself carried Septan back to the ship and put her on a bunk. I checked Dundals hand, It didn't seem too bad but I washed it again to make sure that all the acid was off it. No wonder we'd not seen any animals around! We blasted off, wondering if we ought to land on any more planets. Septan was recovering but it had been touch and go for awhile, shock, the pain then a fever we didn't know anything about, had left her very weak. She had us worried for weeks. She wouldn't be able to use her hand ever again. Moral was at a low, though I hadn't wasted the weeks. I had been learning to fly a spaceship! I still made mistakes but on the whole , I was pretty well pleased with myself! Dundal and Septan were sleeping and I was on station (as us space types say) when we were jumped by a couple of fighters. I jabbed at the button that kicked in the ships defences when we suddenly stopped dead! I shot forward and hit the console, banging my knees, I said a few short words on the subject, then shot back into the seat again! I tried again and this time hit the right button. Dundal came into the control room, rubbing his head and shoulder.

"What happened?" he asked, he used some other words but I ignored those.

"I don't really know, two fighters appeared out of nowhere and I went to put the defences on auto. I guess I hit the wrong button and we just stopped. "

He looked at the button I'd hit and started laughing!

"What's the joke, come on tell me. What does it say?" I asked.

I still couldn't read most of the Uxtomal figures.

"It'e the reverse thrust button, that's why they didn't fire on their first pass. When we stopped they over shot us."

He came out with a lot of Jargon about how, with the fighters over shooting, It would take them about ten minutes to catch up with us. He sat down and started pressing buttons. The ship turned round and

31

then increased speed away from the fighters. We watched our radar screen, from behind a large asteroid appeared the Xiobarg mothership, Dundal was quite confident we could out run them, apparently, the fighters only had a short range.

"I think we had better try another corner of space. It seems to be getting crowded here. " he said.

I asked him why he seemed so cheerful?

Septan is asking for food and I think I know where we are. "I'm not absolutely sure but I think I recognise some of these star charts. " Well! I just sat there and stared at him with my mouth open!

"You mean we're not lost anymore?" I said.

"Oh I didn't say that. Don't Forget the Uxtomal ship we were on will have been ransacked by the Xiobargs and any information in the computer will have been transferred to their own ship. Even if we find my own planet the chances are the Xiobargs and Uxtomals will be fighting over it! " He said.

"That also means the Xiobargs will have the location of my own world. Christ, it wont stand a chance against them"! As I thought about the prospect of this happening, my newly arisen hopes dropped lover than a snakes arse! I looked at Dundal, he was obviously thinking about his own world.

"Which way are we going to go, we could end up in a battle which ever way we go! Have you any ideas?"I hoped he had because I hadn't!

Suddenly he said

"One thing is for certain, if the Xiobargs have the location of all those planets then We can't warn anybody because we don't know where we are and we can't stay in this galaxy because we would soon end up dead! The only thing we can do is head for another galaxy as far away as possible. Preferably without any Xiobargs or Uxtomals, He looked at me blankly, then I said.

"Then what happens?'

"We live!

We sat there just thinking. Dundal had set a course away from the danger area and he now put the ship back on auto pilot. We were brought out of our day dreaming by the arrival of Septan in the control room

"What's the matter with you two, you look as if someone special had just died!" She said.

We told her what we had been discussing, all she said was oh! , them she sat down and the same look that was on our faces soon appeared on hers. We couldn't fight, we couldn't warn anyone. We couldn't stay in this galaxy, all we could do was run, we didn't like this but there wasn't a lot we could do about it. Dundal said he would stay on watch so I went to my cabin. I laid down on the bunk and gradually fell asleep. I was dreaming. We were surrounded by hundreds of huge ships, Xiobargs on one side, Uxtomale on the other. They were firing at each other and we were in the middle! I was shouting and waving my arms but it was as though no one could see or hear me! My actions were getting more and more desperate when I suddenly woke up! My heart was hammering fit to bust and I was wet through, I was still half asleep as I groped my way to the shower. I was in there about an hour! I gradually got it together and after having a drink I went forward to the control room. Dundal was still on duty and I asked it everything was alright. He assured me that everything was fine with the ship but that he was still depressed. He had been going over our situation in his mind and he couldn't find any kind of solution. Septan came in and she admitted that she too had been

thinking but that she couldn't see any other course of action but the one we were taking. The only thing to do now was to choose a direction in which to head. We were discussing this when I asked if the computer had stored the information about the two Xiobarg attacks on us. Dundal pressed a few buttons and upon the screen appeared a display showing our travels since we had left the Uxtmal mothership. There were the planets we had landed on and the position and the two attacks. I suggested we head anywhere away from these locations and, after a little thought, Dundal and Septan agreed. We sort of tossed a coin and picked a direction. We needed to locate a planet where we could relax and give the outside of the ship a going over. I was a little bit skeptical about this and with good reason; the planets we had so far landed on had been none too friendly Septans arm had healed but so far, it was unusable.

We sailed, flew, cruised or what ever it is that spaceships do, for about two months with nothing to relieve the boredom but sleep, when early one morning, the alarm sounded! I shot out of my cabin in a panic heading for the control room. I burst in to find Septan and Dundal already there. They gave me an amazed look, then carried on as if nothing had happened!

"What's going on, are we under attack, or what?" I asked.

They gave a condescending look, it was Dundal who eventually explained after they had calmed me down. they had been doing some changes to the ships computer and also translating the Uxtomal writing to theirs.They had also fitted an alarm to the sensors to warn of an approaching planet. I pointed out that they had failed to warn me and that they had rightened me out of ten years growth! Septan said she didn't believe me because she knew from studies made of my planet that I had stopped growing years ago! When I tried to explain it was a joke she just stared at me as if I was mentally retarded! I don't think the communication boxes or translator modules as Dundal informed me, helped as they couldn't convey the tone or inflection needed. Some of the translations were weird to say the least! The computer was flashing like mad, Dundal and Septan could read it but I hadn't a clue, as usual! Dundal spoke to me.

"Well David," it came out more like "Daazqeed"but I knew what he meant

"We seem to have found an acceptable planet on which to rest and repair any damage."

Thats what all the flashing lights were for!

"That's great Dundal but lets not count our chickens eh?" I said

"We haven't any chickens?" this was Septan.

"Forget it, we haven't the time."

How can you explain something like a sense of humour that's taken hundreds of years to develop to a couple of aliens in easy stages through a translator that everything comes out of in one flat monotone, IMPOSSIBLE! I said.

"Lets fly round it a few times first and give the sensors a chance to pick anything up?" So I was being cautious, but after the other planets, I had a right to be! Our scanners showed life forms but not what type. They could be harmless or they could be dangerous, we wouldn't know till it was too late. A vote was taken and it was decided that we would land. I won't tell you which way I voted! The sensors did tell us that the planet would support our type of life at least we would be able to breath without suits. We landed close to some pretty impressive cliffs. Dundal studied them for hours, then he spoke at some length to Septan. The pair of them got a couple of rifles and under Dundals instruction they started enlarging the existing caves. This went on for a full day. When Dundal was satisfied with the number of rooms he had, he started to melt the rock to leave a smooth finish. While he was doing this part of the job, Septan was using the ships computer to sample the soil and any rocks that we brought her. She found a substance that when subjected to extreme heat ' turned into glass. I, of course, had the most technical job of all; moving all the rubble and rubbish! A couple of weeks past and I kept getting the impression that I wasn't wanted. I would walk into conversations that ended abruptly with Dundal and Septan looking sheepish, well as sheepish as two cats can! One of the conversations was "We can farm the local fauna and flora and we'll have some of the ships stores as a back up and. . " It was at this point that I walked into the room. There was an embarrassed silence for a few moments, then I said.

"So you are staying here then?"

As soon as I said it I thought, what a stupid and obvious thing to say. Of course they're staying, what else was all the work.for. They looked even more abashed but they did invite me to stay, if I wanted to. They were about as sincere as a taxman, saying I won't take much!

"If you help me stock up with fresh food I will leave you two love birds to your new planet"

"It's all stocked up ready, the water has been replenished as well. "

Septan said this all in one go then blushed. Well, at least they weren't trying to rush me! I didn't like long goodbyes but well, I felt about as welcome as a fart in a space suit!

"Oh! Ah! Yes, well I may as well get er, going then."

Within a few minutes, I was on board and Dundal was giving me some final instructions.

"Septan has reprogrammed the computer to react to your voice and it shouldn't take you long to change anything we have forgotten." I was trying to think of things, but they'd thought of everything, there wag no reason for me to delay any longer. Dundals last words to me really cheered me up. "We wish you luck David, Septan has programmed the computer to erase any logs of this planet and the journeys too and away from it so you need not worry about us if you get captured. "

I thanked him for his concern and how much I hoped his and Septans children inherited their parents compassion and selflessness. My sarcasm was, of course, wasted and I felt bad when he thanked me! He held out his paw and said goodbye, After he'd left the ship I closed the airlock. I was feeling lonely already! Then I thought SOD EM! I'll show them what us Earthmen are made of!

"Computer, on my command, get ready to blast off."

I checked the view screen to make sure they were out of the way then I strapped myself into my seat and gave the command that sent me out into the unknown. I thought of the star trek caption To boldly go where no men have gone before, no men only homicidal aliens!

Chapter – 3

Well here I was flitting around in outer space, not a clue where I was or where I was going or for that matter what I was going to do when got there! I spent a couple of weeks doing absolutely nothing, the computer ran everything so I was as much use as a one legged man at an arse kicking contest! I had programmed the computer to play chess but I soon got fed up with that as the computer kept beating me! What I really needed was some one to talk to. I had been talking to the furniture, my reflection would have me saying things like, what are you staring at pal. My actions were starting to worry me My reflection and the furniture were talking back! Suddenly I had a brilliant idea, I wondered if I could programme the computer to talk. I hurriedly sat at the control board for the computer. With some excitement I typed in the question. Can I programme you to talk? Is it possible to do this? What do I have to do or add to your system? As I pushed the answer button I sat back and waited. I didn't have long to wait. Written across the screen were the words If you install a voice simulator. Where the hell was I to get one from! As far as I knew there wasn't a voice simulator on the ship. I sat there for a few hours racking my brains looking all over the control room, my eyes kept coming to rest on a "box". Suddenly I realised what I was looking at. You daft git! I thought. It's been sitting there in front of me all this time I typed in, can a translator module be used. I also fed in a circuit diagram I had found, I waited then. Yes if it was modified first. For the next four hours I plied the computer with questions, then set about modifying the module. Finally it was ready, I had lost my temper a few times and a bit of skin but only one more wire to connect! I couldn't wait! I sat back and reviewed my handy work. I sat there for about ten minutes and nothing had happened! SHIT! SHIT! SHIT! All that work for nothing! Suddenly, I was startled by a strange voice

"This word does not register in my memory bank. "

I felt such a fool! or course, If I didn't speak to the computer first it wouldn't speak to me! My next problem was what to call the computer, I couldn't go on calling it, 'it. I thought I'll be clever, if I gave the computer a list of female names then it could pick one its self. I also instructed the computer to initiate speech and to use the ships sensors to react to my presence. It's a good job I liked watching sci-fi films or I wouldn't have known half of this stuff! I gave it half an hour then asked which name it had picked. I could have saved myself some trouble by not giving it the list, every name it came up with, I rejected. In the end I decided to call it com for short! A couple of days pasted and I thought I'd never get used to the tinny sound of "coms" voice.

I was dreaming that I was out walking the fields with my dog when a farmer came shouting at me. Instead of him shouting, get of my land, he was shouting "Alarm, space craft approaching." this was repeated over and over in a tinny voice. I thought how funny, he's got a voice just like "com. I suddenly realised it was com, then the full impact of what she was shouting hit me. A ship! CHRIST! It could only be an enemy I jumped up and raced to the control room. Showing on the screen was a ship about the same size as mine.

"Identify" I said in as a commanding tone as I could manage. It sounded shaky to me but "com didn't seem to notice.

"Unknown, not Xiobarg nor Uxtomal construction."

I was getting my composure back but before I could say anything "com" spoke.

"It is not of Numal construction either, I am scanning for information, life forms on board also unknown. "" "Can we out run it if it turns out to be hostile?" I asked.

I was only asking as a precautionary measure Well it's best to cover all the angles isn't it,? Well it is!

"Cannot answer, alien ship has star drive as do we. "

Before I could think of an answer "com" continued, "We have superior fire power and defences."

Well now that's different. Just let them try anything and they'd never forget the human race. ARIGHT! Its suprising what effect having a bigger stick than your enemy can do for your ego. Not that I would have run away or anything, but, well, you know what I mean, I…

Just then "com" interrupted my thoughts. Apparently she was receiving a call from the other ship. They had also been scanning us, I bet we didn't compute for them either. It took "com" about fifteen minutes to translate their language so I could understand it, then she put it over the loud speaker.

"Who are you and what are you; and why are you in our space zone?

Identify your self or we will attack. My first reaction was to tell them to sod off! Being bigger gives one an intolerant feeling. Then I thought about it, I just couldn't go swanning around space for ever, I needed help and I was as lonely as hell. I sent this message across.

"I am a Terran from the planet Earth, this is an Uxtomal ship. I was a prisoner of the Uxtomals but escaped when they were attacked by the Xiobargs. I am lost, can you help me?"

After about an hour they replied.

"We do not believe you, We have never heard of any of the races you

have named. We will board your ship, do not resist or you will be destroyed, understood?"

I was gob smacked, of all the cheek! I sent my reply

"Who the hell do you think you are pal! If you check your scanners you will see that I out gun you so don't start some thing you can't finish, That told them by God!" I then told them.

"You can send one crew member over but be warned, if he is armed in an way, I will destroy your ship. Understand? Oh by the way, I hope you are oxygen breathers because I am. "

Bloody aliens, think they own the place. Well we'll see about that.

After about half an hour they replied. "We didn't mean any harm!" They'd obviously checked their scanners."We are Bloorans from the planet Jaral of the Aboorian system. We are also oxygen breathers. One of our crew will come across to your ship to assist you."

I told "com" to scan the shuttle for weapons and to make sure there was only one of them on board. While I awaited my visitor, I tried to imagine what they looked like. Were they reptilian, slug like or maybe they were like insects or a blob of jelly. I was frightening myself! It sometimes doesn't pay to have an imagination! "Com" flashed up a picture on our screen of the inside of the alien shuttle. I recieved a shock! The alien looked like me! Humanoid! I asked "Com" for a read out on the alien.

"Scanners show similar life form to your self. "

"What's happening now com. "

"Shuttle next to airlock, alien leaving shuttle, now entering airlock, outer door on air lock closed. Normal gravity, inner airlock door open. alien entering ship. "

I was watching the monitor as the alien removed its helmet. I don't know what I was really expecting but I was still shocked when I saw the colour. The alien was a deep blue and coupled with a bald head, well I just stood there flabbergasted. Not even the pointed ears got to me as much as the bald blue head. It stood there staring at me, and me with my mouth wide open at that! I finally came round and asked Com if I could talk with it. Apparently Com had already translated my first words so the next thing was to apologise for calling it an it and ask its name. The alien looked startled for a bit then said.

"I am called. " It sounded like Charlie to me. "We wish to know why you have invaded our space zone and what your intentions are?"

"First things first, I'm not invading your space and my intentions are peaceful. I'm lost as I said before. Iv'e never heard of your race or planet before now. All I want is some help to get home to my own world ,where ever it is."

Charlie started speaking.

"If you are telling the truth, then we will help you all we can. As far as I know, we have never heard of your planet. In what system does it lay, how far is it away?"

I hadn't a clue! I explained again how I had ended up in their space but even to me it sounded far fetched. We past a few more questions between us before Charlie said he'd got to get back to his ship and report. As Charlie was on his way to the airlock I asked Com for a readout on the physical aspects of the alien. Com told me that the internal structure differed but little from my own. The big shock was that Charlie was't a him but a she It was while I was digesting this latest info and Charlie was still in the air lock that Com delivered the biggest shock so far.

"Alert, two alien craft approaching, unknown design. Alarm they have opened fire. "

BLOODY HELL! before I could say anything Com continued.

"All defences are on maximum, weapons ready."

"Put the screens on Com. " at last I had found my voice.

I didn't know it but Charlie had come back to the control room and as the screens came on we were in time to see Charlies ship blow up. It wasn't till she gasped, that I realised she was there. The Bloorans had returned fire because one of the enemy ships was just laying there. I looked at Charlie, she was just staring at the screens. I grabbed her by the arm and shaking her I asked who the new lot were. She was still in shock but said.

"They are unknown to me, We have newer seen a ship like that before! "

"Com scan them, see if you can find out who they are.

I had just finished speaking to Com when she reported that the remaining enemy ship was turning towards us . We watched on the screens, suddenly they opened fire, Com took evasive action and fired back. This went on for about twenty minutes with each ship scoring slight hits but doing no real damage. I was getting fed up with this.

"Com put the forward guns on manual, lets me have a shot at him."

Com tried to advise against it but I was adamant. All this predicted computer stuff was getting me down and besides which the enemy could have called up reinforcements. I got com to give as much power to the

guns as she could with out taking any away from the shields. As the alien ship passed us I raked him from stem to stern. I got him, he went spinning out of control. Com told us that I'd scored a hit on their drive unit resulting in a total loss of power. That will show the s.o b. I asked Com if she had identified the enemy ships yet. she had, they were Xiobarg ships and the ship I had disabled still had life forms on it.

Her recommendation was to destroy both ships totally to leave no trace.

I looked at Charlie.

"I thought that the Xiobargs were unknown to you?" I asked.

"They are, i've newer heard of them before. "

She was still in a daze. Com offered the only logical explanation. The Xiobargs had followed us!

"How is that possible, " I was a bit bewildered. " What did they use, long range scanners or what? We've been wandering around space for ages?" Com then went into a rather lengthy explanation on used matter and photons from a star drive. What it all boiled down to was that we were like a ship at sea and the Xiobargs had followed our wake. Com came on again

"Suggest we destroy Xiobarg ships immediately.

"Why Com? They can't hurt us, the've no power."

"One is sending a distress call which I am blocking, they both can be detected on long range scanners. Others may come. "

"I can't fire on a defencless ship, its not right. What harm can they do to us? Why don't we just fly away?"

"When the others arrive the surviving aliens will send them after us."

I then had a horrible thought. It was of a whole fleet of Xiobarg ships coming into this region of space and wiping every living thing in it! And I would be responsible! GOOD GRIEF! I suddenly remembered Dundal and Septan. What if the Xiobargs had followed us to that planet. They would have destroyed it. The more I thought about it the madder I got. It was the bloody Xiobargs that needed exterminating! With that thought in mind I sat down at the gun controls and told Com to give me maximum power. I sighted on the ship which was sending the distress call, and I let it have it! I didn't stop till Com told me that even this close she couldn't pick up anything of it on the scanners. I did the same with the other ship. The damaged Blooran ship we decided to salvage and with it in tow we set out for Charlies home planet. We had to go slowly as we had to put maximum power into our tractor beam. Charlie had regained some of her composure by this time and was asking questionas

"Who are the Xiobarg5? Why aid they attack us?"

"Believe me when I tell you they are homicidal maniacs, and you don't want to meet one face to face! Com, that distress call, did you jammed it?"

"Yes, the only thing another ship will hear is static. "

Well that was good news. I relaxed little and asked Charlie to give Com the location of her home world. While she did that I went to get something to eat. After all the excitement, I also needed to use the toilet! The trip to Charlies world proved to be uneventful. I was in the control room as we neared Jaral and the closer we got the more ships appeared. Com gave all the right responses to the Blooran challanges, supplied, of course, by Charlie. After leaving the damaged ship in orbit we landed at the main space port. I was a bit apprehensive about leaving the ship but Com assured me she wouldn't let anyone else on board

while I was outside. As I left the ship I was met with the sight of nothing but blue bald heads with pointed ears! The Bloorans didn't make a sound, they just stared at me. They parted to let a group of about twenty through and they told me they were to escort me to a building where I would be given food and drink. I'd taken one of the boxes with me so I could make myself understood. After I had rested and eaten I asked one of the guards where Charlie was but he either didn't know or didn't want to know. A Blooran entered the room where I was and started to question me.

"Who are you and where do you come from? Who attacked our ship and why. Are there more of them? Where do they come from and why did you, an alien, bring our ship back?"

I said, more to myself, he'd be wanting my grandmothers inside leg measurement next He asked me what I'd meant by that. I said forget it. I started from the first day and went right through my story. After I'd finished, he seemed shocked. He asked me to wait and he left the room. He'd been gone a good hour when he retuned, but this time he wasn't alone. He'd brought six others with him. After he had introduced them he asked me to repeat my story. After I had, they all looked shocked! There was silence for ages then they all wanted to talk at once. The one who had come to see me on my own must have been the leader because when he called for silence he got it straight away. He turned to me and said.

"We have not had any fighting in this system for hundreds of years. We know of other life forms and have always found them to be peaceful some we even trade with and have done so for years. Now you turn up with your story of warlike aliens who will fight and kill and destroy for no apparent reason. I do not believe you, I think that you are the dangerous one, I think that you fired on our ship without warning when they challenged you. I also think that because you feared reprisals you concocted this story and brought our ship back to help make us believe you.

I just sat there, it was my turn to be shocked! They thought I was a pirate or something, they had to be joking! When I looked around the circle of faces I realised that they wern't. DEEP SHIT! What was I going to do, I had to think and fast! Of course Charlie, she could verify my story, but where was she?I told them to find her but they just stared at me. Before any of them could say anything else I said.

"One of your ships crew came across to my ship just before the attack and if you find her she will confirm what I have told you! You can also check my ships computer. "

I then sat back and tried to appear unconcerned and I put what I hoped was a bored expression on my face. I hoped they didn't come too close to me as in times of stress one is liable to generate a lot of gas! They spoke amongst themselves for a while, one of them used a communicator and in a short while the door opened and there was Charlie, Man was I ever glad to see her! I think my voice betrayed my outward appearance

"Charlie, you've got to tell them what really happened, they think I a bloody pirate for Gods sake"

She looked at ma for a moment, nodded then turned to the leader and said; "What the Terran says is true Lord, I had just reached his ship when we were attacked. My own crew were killed, we destroyed the aliens and brought back my ship for repair.

She had started to cry when she mentioned her shipmates. At least I took the noise she was making to be crying. It was all rather weird. There were some funny sounds coming from the rest of the gang as well! I sat there, too relieved to do anything else. The leader asked tor silence

again then turned to me and in a differant tone to the previous one started to ask questions again.

"We are sorry we misjudged you, please forgive us."

I said think nothing of it.

"How long do you think it will be before the, Xiobargs is it? How long before they enter our system? how many are there?"

I could only answer, I don't know to both questions. I told them I'd tried to cover my trail but if their equipment was half as good as I thought it was, It wouldn't be long. This caused another stir amongst them. I grabbed the leader by the arm and said,

"If I were you I'd alert the whole planet and put everybody on standby to evacuate. Send a couple of your fastest scout ships to watch for the Xiobargs and send others out to warn any other races you know of.

While he was telling his people what to do I took Charlie to one side and tried to pump her for information.

"Charlie, do your people have any big ships to fight with, really big ones because the Xiobargs do, I have seen one."

"The only ones we have are about half as big again as yours Time to panic! My bowel muscles will never be the same. When I explained to Charlie what I meant by big she went white, and I mean white! If I'd put a wig on her head she would have passed as human! Slowly the colour returned to her face and she said in a quiet voice.

" I had better inform our leader, we have nothing to match a ship of that size." Before she turned away I said.

"Tell him he can access my ships computer for any information on the Xiobargs that it holds, if it will help, He's more than welcome. She thanked me then turned to him. As she was speaking to him, he looked over her shoulder at me and nodded. Well I thought, I'd better get ready to leave, it won't be long before this planet is a very noisy place to be. I started to walk towards the space port when Charlie came running up to me.

"Where are you going! " she asked as she fell in step,

"I'm getting out of here and if your people have any sense at all thy will do the same, you can't fight them."

"Where will you go?" She asked.

"Anywhere there isn't an Xiobarg or Uxtomal. I will have to find a planet

I can live on as I don't think I will ever find my own. "

She looked thoughtful for awhile then said.

"Can I come with you, theres nothing for me here and my people will be leaving anyway?"

I just stopped in my tracks! I turned to look at her and thought why not. She's no different to Earth women. I knew loads of blue, bald, pointed eared women on Earth, who didn't.

"Ok, lets go. I'm not promising anything, it could be years before we find a suitable planet. "

Ag we climbed aboard my ship, I was happier than I had been in a long time. I had found a companion! Bye bye blues, excuse the pun. As we blasted off I told her about the longevity drug Id been injected with. She got a bit down at the thought of growing old but cheered up slightly when I said I'd ask Com if I could make a serum out of my blood. She said we didn't have to, as there was a supply of the drug in the medical room.

We both cheered up at this and we set off for the dispensary. While we were in there Com told us some sobering news. She had been monitoring signals and it seemed the Blooran world wags under attack! The Bloorans were holding their own against the Xiobarg fighters, but that she could detect the mothership at extreme sensor range. I asked if we were in any danger, Com assured me we weren't. No scanners were being directed in our vicinity. That was good news, maybe they would keep fighting long enough for us to get away. I instructed Com to go to maximum speed and soon we were well out of range. I felt better but Charlie was upset. She was like this for a week, she hardly ate, she didn't talk, she just moped about. In the end I lost my temper with her and started shouting and insulting her. I told her I wished I'd never brought her with me as she was as much use as a chocolate fireguard!

She looked at me in shock then burst into tears making me feel a right bastard! I mumbled apologise, said I hadn't meant what I'd said and blushing like mad I fled to my cabin! During the next few days we didn't speak, I'd been working in the control room and one of the things I had fitted was a film of plastic over the screens and I had marked it into sections. I'd programmed Com with the new information and done various other little things. On the eleventh day out from Jaral the alarm went. Com came on.

"Ships approaching, from sector 3, six Blooran ships and four unidentified, password used on Jaral being transmitted to them. "

After a slight pause Com said.

"Password correct, putting the commanders message on screen now. "

Up on the view screen came a blue face. He identified himself as one of the officers present when I had been interviewd by his leader. He told us that as far as he knew his ships were the only ones to get away before the Xiobarg mothership had arrived. I asked about the four unidentified ships and was told that they were Blooran freighters packed with civilians. He told us how he had watched as his worlds cities and towns were destroyed. I asked him what he would do now?

"We will travel into deep space and try to find a planet suitable to colonise, would you like to come with us?" He asked.

The offer was very tempting, I looked at Charlie, she just pointed at me as if to say it's your choice. I looked back at the screen.

"No thanks, I think well just travel for a while, see some of the stars, ok?"

"Very well. I hope you realise that you would stand a better chance with us. "

"Yes, I realise we probably would but your going int the wrong direction for us. Good luck in your search."

As the screen went blank I turned to Charlie.

"Well were really on our own now. One good thing though, if the Xiobargs come this way they will be able to follow them easier than us."

"What do you mean?" Charlie looked aghast!

"Well it stands to reason that they will follow them because they'll leave the bigger trail, I hope."

"You hope. You want them to get caught?"

"No of cause not! But we don't want the Xiobargs to follow us do we and its obvious that they will look for survivors. Com set a course that will take us across the Bloorans. Hopefully we can loose our energy trail in theirs. "

We crossed over their ships trail and set off into deep space at right angles to them. Com had fired us at full speed then shut down our engines so we wouldn't leave a trail; we coasted on for about an hour then Com fired us up and we set off into regions unknown; We had been getting on each other nerves for about a week earth time, when Com called us to the bridge.

"We are approaching a planet which is capable of supporting Blooran and Earth life forms. "

I let out a sigh of relief, I had had visions of Xiobargs attacking, I turned to Charlie and asked.

"Have you any idea where we are? Have your people ever visited this system?"

She looked at the screen and checked the instruments before replying.

"I don't think so, it doesn't look familiar. "

I asked Com to scan the planet for any life forms, Any really big ones. Coms reply that there was life but as yet unidentifiable, left me feeling uneasy. I looked across at Charlie and asked.

"Should we chance it. Should we land and have a look around?

"We might as well, we might just be able to live there. It could be ages before we found anything else. "

As we got closer, the more uneasy I felt. Maybe it was too soon and the doubts about having lost the Xiobargs kept coming back. They were only a couple of weeks away. I was also frightened that Charlie might get killed. Not mainly for her sake but mine, I'd be on my own, again!

Suddenly Com's voice filled the control room.

"Ruined city below showing signs of heat radiation,

"Prom fires or heating units?" I asked

"Heat from residue of energy beams . Less then one week old. Life forms possible survivors of attack,"

"Get us out of here Com, as fast as you can. Full scan for other ships, maximum range."

The Xiobargs must have been here. For the next few hours I was on edge, I finally calmed down enough to notice that Charlie was giving me dirty looks!

"What's wrong with you now?" "You think we should have landed and tried to help those people."

"You don't think we should, do you.? " she said.

She tried to say something else but I carried on.

"What do you think would have happened to us if we had landed, ?" Before she could reply I said.

"I'll tell what. We would have exhausted our medical supplies in the first hour. Then if we were lucky, we would have blasted off. If not, this ship would have been swamped and ransacked for food and we would have in all probability, been killed. I am not risking my ship just to please you. You want to help then I will go back and drop you off! " I had gradually been raising my voice and as I shouted this at her, she shook her head and dabbed at her tear filled eyes. In a quiet voice she asked me what was running through my mind, where too now?

"I don't know, I don't know where we are or where we have been for that matter. Tell you what, you pick a course, anywhere as long as it's not backwards! " with that I turned round and sat down in one of the console chairs. Charlie told Con to carry on the way we were going for the time being. It was as good as anything. We hadn't been travelling too long before

Com frightened the life out of me again!

"Ships approaching fast from the rear. "

"Can you tell us who they are Com, are they Xiobargs?"

I thought this is probably the end, I was scared. Then I started to get mad. Bloody Xiobargs! Who the hell do they think they are Why can't they leave us alone for Gods sake!

"What are you mumbling about?" Charlie asked.

Charlie was staring at me, before I could have a go at her Com came back on,

"Identified. They are Blooran ships, three of them, all have sustained damage. " I just let out a big sight What a relief !

"Com put all defences on maximum and arm all weapons ready to fire." Charlie looked at me in horror!

"But they are my people, you can't fire on them! "

"Theyv'e obviously met up with the Xiobargs. "

"How do you know that, you can't possibly know that. "

"Charlie, think. Why are there only three ships and they are damaged. What if the Xiobargs captured the ships and they are full of their soldiers. Isn't it better to be careful rather than be sorry?"

Charlie was quiet and I could see she was thinking about what I had said.

"Scanners show Blooran survivors on board, no other forms of life."

That was a relier not only to Charlie but to me!

"Com put me through to the Bloorns ships and scan behind them to see if there being followed. "

Com scanned but couldn't detect anything, except an energy trail a blind man could follow. They had been going flat out. I got through and asked to speak to the leader.

"Our leaders are dead, killed by the Xiobargs. Can we come with you?"

They sounded more scared than me! After chewing my lip for awhile it dawned on me what he'd said, They wanted me to lead. To be the leader!

"Yes, right. The first thing we do is to throw off any persuit and we do this by going to full speed for six hours then we will shut of the engines and let our forward motion carry us on. At a slight angle to the original course. This should give us a chance to treat any wounded you have on board. Anybody got any objections or bettor ideas?"

Nobody had so we followed my plan. While we drifted I asked the Bloorans what kind of damage, if any, their ships had sustained. Only one ship had serious damage and as we progressed it was getting worse. As we were passing near a large asteroid belt I suggested the crew of the ship should abandon it amongst them. We spread the crew amongst our remaining three ships, this was all carried out without mishap, and then we carried on.

Once beyond the asteroid belt we put full power on hoping that the belt would mask our trail. On and on we travelled with out meeting any new planets or any sign of the Xiobargs. I was in the shower when the alarm went, and as I reached the control deck, I was just in time to see the picture that Com flashed on to the screen. In front of us was a fleet of the biggest ships I had ever seen.I asked Com.

"Who are they , where did they come from?"

"Unknown. scanners being blocked, they are scanning us."

Suddenly the picture on the screen changed. A face appeared and it looked human! I was a little taken aback at that! Then the alien spoke

" Who are you and where are you from?"

I just stood there with my mouth hanging open.

"Why don't you answer?" demanded the face.

"What, What did you say?" I replied stupidly.

"Who are you and where are you from?" He was getting angry.

"I'm an Earthman and the rest of us are Bloorans. We are trying to escape from the Xiobargs who have destroyed the Blooran world. "

"We will board your ship and check your computer tapes, do not try to resist or you will be vaporised. Do you understand?"

Before I could reply the screen went blank, I turned to Charlie and she gave me a funny look. I asked.

"What's the matter Charlie?"

"They look exactly like you. " she said.

To give myself time to think I asked Com if our scanners were still being blocked. She confirmed this and also informed us that a shuttle was on its way over and would be docking shortly. I sat down to wait. When Com told us the aliens were in the air lock I told her to put their picture up on the screen, When she had done it took me a second glance to be sure, then I burst out laughing. I couldn't stop, I was rolling about on the floor. Charlie was shouting, " What was wrong with me, was I ill? When I eventually managed to get myself under control I got to my feet only to collapse again when I saw the alien standing in the doorway! It was about five minutes before I could stand and even then I was having difficulty in keeping a straight face. You see the alien was only about two and a half foot tall! The look on his face was one of shock. I don't think he liked our size. He must have wondered what he had got his self into. I opened the conversation by introducing myself,

"Welcome, my name is David, I'm an Terran and this is Charlie, she's a Blooran and you are?"

He didn't answer. I asked Com if she had translated and before she could answer, the alien said that he had understood everything we had said. He said that he had been studying us. He told us he was from a race called Cammeels. He told us his name was Lank. I collapsed again, four or the Bloorans carried me to my quarters and put me on my bunk. When I had fully recovered, my ribs hurt like hell, I went back to the control room. The Camaeel was just finishing with Com as I entered and he gave me a quizzical look. I sat down before saying.

"It's a medical condition that only affects humans. Did you get all the information you require?"

"Yes, but it doesn't say how you came to be on this ship?"

I told him my story and for a few minutes he just sat there, then the questions started quick and fast.

"Where are the Xiobargs now? Were they following us? What kind of ships and weapons did they have and what were we planning to do? Where were we going to go?"

"Whoa slow down. All the don't knows, are everything you have just asked me. As to where we are going, that's easy to answer, anywhere the Xiobargs and Uxtomals are not . I will tell you one thing, the Xiobargs shoot first then talk so don't waste any time trying to negotiate. " I had better get back to my ship and let the others know and also warn my home world. " He said and was on his way when I asked about us.

He just said he would let us know his decision when he had gone through our computer records. Till then we'd just have to wait. While we waited , we carried out some repairs, and saw to our injured. It was two days before we heard from the

Cammeel commander. While the news wasn't bad, it still wasn't good. We were ordered to move away from the Cammeel space zone. We would get no help from them whatsoever. I was a little annoyed at this treatment and I called the Canmeel commander, Lank.

"What are you hoping to achieve by refusing to help us? The Xiobargs won't just ask where we have gone, They will attack you! Don't you understand that? We need medical help and supplies. "

"My council has told me what to do, I'm sorry but those are my orders. " he replied.

I was fuming. Trying to keep a hold on my temper, I told him that there was noway we were going back the way we had just come. That left me with left or right! I made my mind up and ordered a ninety degree right turn. As we were leaving I couldn't resist a dig at him.

"If you ever find yourselves short handed or under manned don't call us." There was no reaction from him whatsoever! I kid you not, aliens have no sense of humour! He did do one thing though, he sent one of his ships to parallel our course. He was making sure we didn't enter their space. I turned to Charlie with a smug smile on my face but when she asked me why, I just said forget it. We had been travelling about a

week when, after a sleep period, I noticed that the Cammeel ship had gone. I asked Com what had happened."They received a message from the command ship. They left at full speed as the fleet was under attack. The enemy had been identified as Xiobargs and they had tried to communicate with them. There were only two enemy ships so the Cammeels thought that as they out numbered them they would talk. The Xiobarges attacked straight away and before the Cammeels knew what was happening, two of their ships were destroyed an another badly damaged. Both the Xiobarg ships were blown up but several of the single seater fighters got away.

l had told them what to expect! Why hadn't they listened. The shit would really hit the fan now! I felt sorry for the Cammeels and I wished I hadn't been so short with Lank. I told Com to get us out of there fast! I hoped Lank and his people could stop the Xiobargs but I was not very confident. They seemed unstoppable! We fled onwards, the two Blooran ships keeping close station. For weeks we ate, slept and ran. We passed planets and worlds we could have stopped at but they all seemed too close to the Xiobargs, I wasn't sleeping at all just lately and only picking at my food, it was Charlie who brought me out of what was becoming a blue funk, I was getting paranoid!

"David, are we ever going to stop running?"

"What do you mean? When we find the right kind of planet we will stop. "

"We have passed worlds we could have landed on, we need fresh water and food is getting short, we need fresh food! "

She stepped back with a look of shock on her face as I barked.

"We have plenty of food and water, we don't need to stop. They might catch us, we have to keep going. "

I was mumbling to myself when Charlie said she was sorry. I felt a jab in my arm and as I slipped into a deep sleep, I heard her say, It's for your own good, When I came round, I was laying on my bunk. I felt really good, relaxed and refreshed although I was starving! I got up and went to the galley. There was fresh greens and what looked like a roast chicken. It didn't taste like chicken though but it was a welcome change. As I was eating, Charlie entered the galley and smiled. She said I looked better for having had a rest, she then apologised for drugging me.

"I'm glad you did, that few hours sleep has done me a power of good. Why are you looking at me like that?"

"That few hours happens to be ten days, we've been on this planet a week! We've stocked up on everything, food and water etc." She was beaming.

She then told me of the events while I been out. Com had intercepted messages from both the Xiobargs and the Cammeels. The Xiobargs had been stopped by Lank and his ships, the Xiobargs had called for reinforcements. We were safe for the moment. Charlie had decided to land on this planet while we had the chance. The other two ships had nearly completed their repairs. Charlie wanted to stay and she was trying to convince me but, I wasn't sure. The call for help from the Xiobargs only served to make me more uneasy. I went along with Charlie and agreed to have a look around just to please her. As we got to the ramp there was a commotion outside. thinking we were being attacked, my worst fears came flooding back. One of the Bloorans came rushing up babbling like a madman. He was talking too fast for the box to keep up. When we finally got him calmed down he told us that one of his crewmen who had been working on the top of his ship had suddenly collapsed and fallen to the ground. He was babbling about the air being poisonous as he led us to where his man was laid. There wasn't a doctor on any of the ships so, as leader, it was my job to see to him. I got

him carried back to my ship and had Com scan him For injuries. His breathing was ok and Com only found a broken leg So with Coms and Charlies help I set that and then we put his leg in splints. When the man had come around I asked him what had happened. He told us that when his captain had told him to check the top of the ship he had asked it someone else could do it but his captain had ordered him up there. He had only just got up there when he felt funny. He didn't remember anything else. I started to laugh. Charlie asked what was the matter and I told her.

"That captain thinks the air is poisoned or worse. All this man is suffering from is a broken leg and a fear of hight's. On my world its called virtigo. A couple of weeks rest and he'll be fine. We repaired our ships and rested for a few more days then Com called us to the control room. She'd intercepted a message from the Cameel defenders to their home world. They couldn't hold the Xiobargs any longer. We had been enjoying ourselves, relaxing, with no stress. I think we all realised that it was all over Till the Xiobargs were defeated we wouldn't be safe whereever we went. We packed as much fresh food and water into the ships as we could and lifted off into the wild blue yonder. We had been travelling a couple of days when Com intercepted another Cammeel message. This was from the home world telling Lank to hold off the Xiobargs while they prepared to Dime warp. I asked both Com and Charlie what a Dine warp was but neither knew. Com was the only one to offer a realistic answer.

"The only logical explanation is a leap between dimensions."

"If that's possible, any idea how it works Com?" I asked

"Insufficient data. Xiobargs are winning the battle. The Cammeels have four ships remaining wait." We waited about twenty minutes before Com came on again.

"Cammee1 ships have just completed the Dime warp after receiving all clear from home planet. Signals indicate Xiobargs confused as to what happened."

"How old is this news com, How long does it take for the signals to reach us?" I asked

I only asked out of curiosity, I wished I hadn't

"A week of earth time. " While we had been resting on that planet and then cruising about, the Xiobaras could be right behind us. We had taken no precautions since we had met the Cammeels and the Xiobargs could even now be on our trail. I told Com to take us to maximum speed for ten hours then to turn off our course and to drift. When the Blooran captains were told what we were doing and why they began to panic. They wanted to know where we were going. My reply was anywhere the Xiobarg" wern't, whereever that was! Over the next days I had been working with Com, I asked her to scan any planet or asteroid we passed for lead or the elements needed to make it. Within a few days Com had found a planet that had the required metals and chemicals. We circled it and I instructed Com to look for a cave or ravine large enough to take all the ships. We found a large fissure which with a bit of work would suit our needs. I called a meeting of the senior Bloorans and I out lined my plans. They were a bit skeptical but when I told them they could leave if they didn't like it, they came round to my way of thinking. The first job was to level the floor of the fissure so the ships could land, then I sent out parties to fetch back the ores and chemicals we needed. Other teams used blast rifles to cut channels in the rock and to bore out huge boulders into cauldrons. Com worked out the thickness and a safe working width for the lead. We worked like Trojans! We had to fly to another part of the planet to cut trees that we would need for the roof supports and to make a door. It would have to be a huge door to allow our ships in and out. I was using the knowledge I had got from watching all sorts of films back on Earth. We built the roof and lined it with lead, the doors took a little longer. Once the Bloorans got the idea there was no stopping them. The hardest part of the doors was getting the counter balance to work properly. Once that was done we had just about finished our hanger. The Bloorans had complained when I wouldn't let them fit the lead sheets flat on the roof or the door. when I explained the reason they smiled and then set too to complete the job.

Charlie had been working on a special type of glue while we had been building and now it was ready. First you sprayed the glue onto the roof and the door, this was allowed to set. We then gave them another coat of glue then we sprayed the roof and doors with crushed rock. This completely hid our hideout, only one test left. I sent a ship up into space with orders to scan the surface, he was to get lower on each orbit. If he couldn't spot us from half a mile he wouldn't spot us at all. Hopefully, neither would the Xiobargs! We stayed under cover for another couple of days making very thin and light lead capes. If we were caught outside we could cover ourselves with these and hopefully escape detection. At the bottom of our fissure a large plain started.

I assembled a team and we set off to explore. I was hoping to find food, any type would do, animal or vegetable. We had binoculars with us and from our height advantage, we could scan the plain before we got there. We could see a large herd of animals that seemed to be grazing but nothing that seemed to be a danger to us. We moved onto the plain and set off in the direction of the herd. As we neared the animals we passed large holes in the ground, we only gave them a passing glance. The animals in the herd resembled pigs but with long legs and long tails

We crept closer and in a single unit we opened fire. We killed about

two dozen which would last us for weeks and as we watched the others run off I thought that all we needed now was some vegetables and this planet would suit us. I was about to call a ship to pick us and the pigs up when from one of the holes a thing shot out and grabbed one of the Bloorans. It had him by the neck, and then it was gone! It had taken the Blooran with it! We all stood there, rooted to the spot by shock, unable to move. Some of the Bloorans were panicking and this brought me round, I shouted for them to keep still but one or two had turned to run and all but one obeyed my command. The one who had kept running only got so far, he must have passed close to a hole for one minute he was there the next he wasn't! I told everyone to keep away from the holes and to gather around me. No one had seen what had grabbed our shipmate, it had been too fast. I detailed six men to work round to the other side of the hole our comrade had been dragged into, then I and some of the others began throwing the pigs nearer the hole. The creature shot out of its den, even though we were expecting it, it shocked us with it's speed. Luckily, one of the Bloorans was aware enough to shoot it. I shot it again, just to make sure it was dead, before I'd let anyone approach it. It was like a huge snake, at least twenty foot of its body was outside the hole. Nobody wanted to go into it's den to see how long it really was! It's head resembled the pictures I seen of sabre tooth tigers with twelve inch teeth. I didn't hesitate, I got on the radio and told them to bring a ship as we wern't mowing!

We had got over the shock of losing two of our comrades and things were starting to settle down. The pigs weren't bad to eat and camp life was peaceful after the hectic days in space. We had begun to work into the sides of the fissure to enlarge our living space and as supplies were plentiful, we were quite happy. The Xiobargs stopped all that! We had, of course, kept a lookout on top of the cliffs with a portable scanner. He was encased in his lead cape so he couldn't be detected. He

told us of a large ship approaching. I told him to remain on guard and to let us know what was happening. For three days we waited while the ship orbited the planet, then it landed. It landed on the plain and hundreds of Xiobargs began to pour out of it. One or two must have been grabbed by the sabere tooths as every now and then the Xiobargs would fire their weapons into the ground. They also had something else with them! Aliens that neither the Bloorans nor I had ever seen before. These prisoners were soon put to work. They began to build a compound first, and as the days past it became clear they were building a space port.

One of the Bloorans guessed right, it was a forward base for Xiobarg war ships. This meant clearing a huge area of the plain and the Xiobargs had a grim method of killing the sabre tooth snakes, they would surround a hole with blast shields and while they were covered like this, they would tie one of the prisoners to a stake. Then they would move back and begin to make a noise. The snake would attack but because it's victim was tied down it couldn't go back down its hole. The snake didn't kill it's prey straight away, the Xiobargas used to let it pull and tug for some time before finally killing it. They obviously enjoyed listening to the prisoner scream. If a prisoner was still alive they shot him. I think it was this that determined, more than anything else, that we would free the prisoners. While we made plans we had out scouts to monitor the Xiobarg compound. I told the Bloorans about the S. A.S and Commando units of my countryon Earth. One of the Bloorans, his name sounded like Barney, volunteered to sneak into the prisoner compound to find out if they would help from the inside. It was decided that a group of six would be best, they would be under the command of Barney. They would get as close to the work parties as possible and at the end of the day Barney would try to join one of them going back to the compound. The next day we were in position on the slope leading to the plain. One of the Prisoner parties was moving towards us, the party was a mixed one. When the Xiobargs reached one of the snake holes they stopped and then pushed a small figure forward. It took me a second to recognise the figure as a Cammeel. I'd thought they'd all escaped! One of the Xiobargs gave the Cammeel a dagger and pushed him towards the hole. The rest of the Xiobargs stood behind their blast shields. The Cammeel looked around, shrugged then calmly walked into the hole! He wasn't down there long! He came running out and as he came into the open, he shot to the right and headed straight for us! The Xiobargs were thrown into confusion. Some started to follow the Cammeel, this broke their shield wall and just at that moment the snake shot out of its hole. The Cammeel was into the grass and because of his height the snake didn't see him, instead all its attention was attracted by the Xiobargs. It was having a hard time selecting a meal with so much meat on offer, it was striking left, right and centre. It had three down before any of the Xiobargs decided to fire at it! The snake proved an elusive target, it had got another two Xiobargs before they managed to kill it! When the leader had got the situation under control, he sent four guards out to find the Cammeel while the rest of them covered the other prisoners and saw to the wounded guards. Three of then were dead, these the leader ordered the prisoners to bury. The Cammeel had been making steady progress, unknowingly, towards us. He had just stopped to rest when we Jumped him. while we assured him we were real.I got the impression that I had seen him before but that would have to wait till we had disposed of the Xiobarg guards that were nearing our position. One thing about laser rifles, they are silent, nothing above a hiss on stun. I told my men not to fire till I did and only on stun, we would finish off the Xiobargs with knives. We would then dump the bodies down a snake hole, scattering some of their gear abound. we would keep the weapons. This was done with no mishap to our party and with a grateful Cammael.

We returned to our camp. There was no need for Barney to enter the prisoner compound now as we would get the information we needed from the Cammeel. While we were all eating our scouts told us that the leader of the Xiobarg party had trailed his men to the snake hole and having found the evidence we'd placed around must have come to the conclusion that the snakes had killed his men. He had then ordered his remaining men to fire into the hole. This done, the whole party had turned and headed back to the compound. When we finished eating it was time to ask questions of the Cammee1. He told us that there were about three hundred prisoners at the moment, he also told us the Xiobargs treated them poorly, bad food, little water, no sanitation. There was grumbling from the Bloorans at this. Feelings were running high.The vast majority hadn't seen what we had. The Cammee1 gave us detail of the compound and its armament. I was still getting the feeling we had met before and I asked him if we had.He said yes. It was Lank! He was amazed at our camp and after explaining how we had built it he was full of praise for us. I asked him how he came to be captured and he said.

"My ship was just about to Dime warp when we were disabled. The Xiobargs ordered us to surrender or be vaporised. They came aboard and herded the able bodied into shuttles, they shot all the wounded. If they couldn't walk they killed them. "

His voice had been cracking as he finished and Charlie was the first to break the ensuing silence.

"We must rescue the prisoners at once, you must attack the compound. "

"You want the hundred of us to attack about five or six hundred of the enemy. Look in her eyes Barney, See if anybody's in. " Sarcasm is wasted on this lot! Barney just gave me a puzzled look and shrugged to the others. I put my hand on Barneys shoulder and said it didn't matter, forget it. I explained to Charlie that as the enemy out numbered us we would have to be sneaky. We would have to attack at night. With this in mind we would start planning straight away. This calmed Charlie down and I also assured Barney that he would lead the rescue attempt. It was arranged that we would have two strike teams of a dozen men, One would attack the compound defences while the other would attack the Xiobarg ship. Once these were secure the rest of the force would attack the Xiobarg barracks. The team in the compound would also release the prisoners and issue any weapons found or taken. We would keep in touch by short wave radio and we would use our ships if we needed to subdue the barracks. We spent the time up till dark by getting our gear ready. Everybody was involved and we all had a fatalistic attitude about us, it was do or die. No matter what the cost in lives, we had to win. When the time came we set off in our groups to our jump off places. Barney led the compound team while another young officer called Bran led the team attacking the ship. I was leading the main force. Before we left it was also suggested that Barney also have command of a three man team that would try to knock out the radio room. This was vital as we didn't want any more Xiobargs turning up. Barney and Bran's teams were to attack silently if possible, I got my group into position and we waited. he hadn't been there long when one of Barneys men came crawling up to us. Every group had taken a box with them, mainly to talk to the prisoners. One of the team that was to knock out the radio room had over heard the Xiobargs talking to an incoming ship. It was bringing more prisoners and building materials, also a change of guards. Hurriedly contacting both teams on the radio, I told them to wait and sent the Blooran to explain things and to tell him we were all pulling back to base. We managed to get back to base alright, although I felt a little shivery. we decided to rest first then we would review our battle plans. When I awoke I had a streaming cold! This was all I needed! we didn't get anywhere with our plans, we didn't know how many more Xiobargs there would be or where they would be placed. We ajourned our meeting mainly because I was feeling rotten. By the end of two days, half of the Bloorans were down with flu and by the end of the week everybody had it, except me! I got Com to scan Charlie and Barney and it wasn't long before I was inoculating every body. Within a couple of days people were starting to recover. It was during this period that I had a brilliant ideal I called the others to a hurriedly arranged meeting. I out lined my plan and waited while the others talked it through. It was agreed we'd try it and a volunteer was called for. We were going to put one of our flu infected men among the prisoners, hopefully within the week every one including the Xiobarge would be so ill with flu that we would be able to walk into the base and take over. We had not been outside since the flu hit us and we got a shock when we did. The Xiobargs had obviously driven the prisoners hard. Most of the plain was leveled, another stockade, larger than the first one, had been erected. There were now three Xiobarg ships and they had enlarged the defences accordingly. This made our plan with the virus more than essential, we couldn't hide nor could we run, we had to fight and we had to win. We had to wait for a work party to come to our side of the plain and two days later one did. As before it was a mixed bunch, mainly Bloorans and Uxtomals with the odd Cammeel and one or two others that non of us had seen before. When one of our men threw a rock into a bush the Xiobarg guards turned to look, the Blooran volunteer silently joined the group. The poor prisoners were so dazed and dejected that none of them reacted in the slightest! The rest of us backed off and then retreated to our camp to wait. It was over a week before our man sent us a signal and we entered the base. The first ones to be infected were the prisoners and the virus had decimated their ranks. Being so badly treated they had no resistance and many were dead. As we left a medical team to inoculate the ones left, the rest of us saw to the Xiobargs. Those that wern't already dead we soon dispatched, that only left the disposal of the bodies. We decided to cremate all the dead. I thought this would be a monumental task, there were over a thousand Xiobarg dead besides the prisoners. Barney took charge and using one of the captured ships he soon disposed of the bodies with the help of its guns. I was worried another Xiobarg ship would arrive but when we accessed the base computer we found that the base commander had radioed his superiors and told them of the virus. They had told him he was on his own, the planet was isolated from now until he called to say it was cured. This was good news indeed! At least we would have time for the infected prisoners to recover. We decided to move everything down from our camp to the compound. The defences would be able to cope with anything barring a mothership. We broke into the store rooms and discovered an abundance of food and weapons. When everyone was better, we loaded up our ships. I was still in command and I chose one of the Xiobarg ships as flag. Barney had command of one of the others and Lank the other. Our original ships went to Bran and the others to two of our ranking officers. We had over a thousand new men to put on our six ships, and after we had assigned everyone a post we were still left with about three hundred men. I hadn't counted the women! I asked Charlie if she would take charge of these and assign so many to each ship as nurses etc. She complained about sexism! Why, she wanted to know, couldn't women have proper responsible post's instead of the menial tasks. Well what could I say!

I had been toying with an idea, it was that we form a ground attack force. I would model it on the lines of the S. A. S and commandos of Earth. I called a meeting of the captains and before she could say anything I asked Charlie to attend. I out lined my idea and after they had agreed I asked for a volunteer to lead the force. Everybody put their hand up, including Charlie. I finally chose Bran. After the others had left I told Bran everything I could and knew about training and the kind of tactics that both of the Earth forces used. I told him he could ask for volunteers through out the fleet. Fleet! six ships! Well it was a start. Two days after Bran put up his posters, we were swamped with applications. If we had accepted them all we wouldn't have had anyone to fly the ships! Charlie got her way, after we had assigned the women posts within the ships Bran ended up with about four hundred recruits. While all this had been going on, the preparations to leave this planet had been taking place, everything was just about ready We had even sent out hunting parties. We had some prisoners of our own, Uxtomals. When I explained to the others what they were like they wanted to kill them there and then. I had only just managed to stop them, this wasn't out of any pity. They were completely harmless so I decided to leave them on this world when we left. We were about to blast off when we got a message that a ship was arriving at the base! Luckily it was only a freighter. I told the others to let it land, you never know, it might be carrying something useful. The crew never knew what hit them, before they could even cough we had them. We didn't take any chances, but we did manage to take a couple of the crew prisoner. When we opened up the cargo spaces we were appalled! They were crammed with prisoners. They were in a terrible state, God knows how long they had been packed in like this.They were suffering from thirst more than anything, and we didn't waste any time in sorting them out. There were about five or six hundred of them and again they were a mixed bunch. I told my men not to bother with the Uxtomals. There were also some fifty dead and quite a who wouldn't make it. These we made as comfortable as possible. This treatment of prisoners did not endear my men to the Xiobarg prisoners.

When they were brought in front of myself and the senior captains, the Xiobarg leader said he would accept our surrender. Well of all the cheek I looked at him and told him that he and his men were all sentenced to death. He laughed, and said that we didn't frighten him. We took them outside and I had my men rig a long armed contraption with a counter balance. Everyone was looking at me gone out. They soon realised what I intended when we all left the compound. After the Xiobarg leader watched his men being devoured by the sabre tooth he wasn't so cocky.

When it came to his turn he asked for a dagger and the chance to die fighting. After thinking about this I finally agreed, We left his feet tied then moved back out of his reach, I threw him a knife and after untying himself he picked up the knife and growled at us. He stretched his arms and then turned to face the snake hole. Then with a look over his shoulder at us he ran and ducking down disappeared down the hole! Within seconds there were shouts, then screams ,then silence, we trooped back to the compound. It was time to leave, the Uxtomals begged us to take them with us. They had no chance, we left them alive and that was all. We disabled the base and the radio, we took all the weapons with us. I didn't expect the Uxtomals to survive and really I didn't want them to. we still had a lot of sick and injured to care for but this could be done while we looked for a safer place to stay.

We were off on our travels again. Instead of being on my own, I now had a force of seven ships and over fifteen hundred crewmen! The freighter had been turned into a hospital ship. I had Com installed in my new ship and everything seemed alright. We plotted a course that would hopefully, take us away from any more Xiobargs, The three ships we had taken from the Xiobargs were cruisers, only a mother ship out gunned us. Some of our new people caught colds but we soon had them back on their feet after giving them the anti flu injection. Over the next few weeks we trained our men and women, we had devised our own communication link. This enabled Com to use any of the ships sensors to relay any messages to the other ships. Bran had been using the main hanger to train his men and Charlie and her nurses were always there too. She was a little upset that she only had the occasional sprain or graze to practice on! The weeks passed and nothing happened. Training continued but at a less hectic pace, the sick and injured had recovered, and everyone carried out their duties more or less on auto pilot. Every fighting ship, apart from my own, had to perform one of two duties One was a forward scout the other was rearguard. It was our rear ship which brought news that shook us all out of our lethargy! Lank happened to be the captain at the time and his ships appearance and his request to come aboard at once caused quite a stir amongst the fleet. I had him sent to my quarters and the story he had to tell was fascinating. I called a meeting of captains and Lank repeated his story.

"Whilst on duty two days ago, I picked up several blips on our scanners at extreme range. At first I thought it was the Xiobargs and with this in mind I tried to lead them away from the main party. We knew that as soon as they spotted us they would attack and being outnumbered, we were aware we wouldn't last long. For hours we turned and twisted but the other ships didn't come any closer. Knowing of the Xiobargs we thought this behaviour strange. I decided to investigate so we headed straight at the alien ships. When we came within hailing distance, I was surprised when we were called. When we put the message on the view screen I was stunned to see an alien face I had never seen before. When the alien spoke he told me he was a Numal and that he had been following us for a week! He would have contacted us sooner but they couldn't figure out why an Xiobarg ship was manned by unknown aliens. I explained what had

befallen all of us and how we came to have our ships. He told me that they also had first hand experience of both the Xiobargs and the Uxtomals. He said that they were from a Numal outpost and that they had been attacked by the Uxtomals. Their settlement had been destroyed and as they tried to return to their home world the Uxtomals had again attacked, driving them away into unknown space. They had travelled for weeks before meeting another race of beings and when they asked for help the other ships had attacked without warning. These they now knew to be Xiobargs. He then asked if they could join us and I told him I would have to ask you. "

We all had questions to ask Lank and when we had finished I asked for suggestions. The only thing they could agree on was that nobody had ever heard of the Numals before. I kept quiet for the moment and let them talk. I finally reached a decision and when I had silence I told the others what we were going to do.

"Lank I want you to go back and tell the Numals that they are welcome to join us and request their leaders to come and see me. "

As Lank left with a smile on his face the others bombarded me with questions. The main thing they were worried about was that the Numals might be as bad as the Xiobargs. I told them what the Uxtomal doctor had told me about them. Barney came out with a poser.

"What if they have changed?"

1 thought for awhile then said,

"We'll let them come in between our ships and if they start anything we will have them in a cross fire. "

There was only one flaw in that plan and it was Charlie who pointed it out. She said, what if they have more ships than us. I just hummed and blew air and then returned to the control room. Com told us the next day that she had the Numal ships on her scanners. I asked her how many there were and Com informed me that there were ten ships besides Lanks. I asked, How big and Com replied that they were different sizes, two were about the same size as a Xiobarg mothership. So much for my plan, they not only out numbered us but out gunned us as well! I informed the captains that in the case of trouble it would be every ship for itself. I also instructed everyone to go to first stage alert. Com informed me that we were being scanned and that as the scanners were so powerful at that range it was safe to assume our signals would also have been picked up. The Numal ships came ever closer and everyone was tense. we received Lanks call to tell us he was leaving his ship to pick up The Numals

We all watched the view screen as his shuttle craft docked at one of the big Numal ships then left it on it's journey to my ship. Suddenly Com flashed up the view inside the shuttle. We all stared at the screen. The Numals had green skin with cats eyes, pointed ears and a stiff brush of hair. I didn't realise I was staring at the screen till Lank shouted.

"Captain, are you receiving me?"

"What, er, yes, er, receiving you loud and clear," I managed to say.

"Permission to come aboard, for the third time." Lank sounded a bit peeved.

"Permission granted, please bring our quests to the board room, I and my senior officers will meet you there" Hopefully I sounded a bit more professional.

Barney was already with me and I asked a crewman to inform Charlie to meet us. I had an honour guard waiting, command ed by Bran, by the airlock when Lanks shuttle docked and they escorted our visitors to the board room. As the Numals entered the room we all stood. At first sight I had thought them tall but I suppose that anyone would look tall next to Lank. They were all about five and a half feet tall, I topped them by a good three to four inches. I pointed to seats around the table and once they were seated I asked if they would care for refreshments. They declined this and seemed a little put out when I and the rest ordered drinks. Charlie was giving the Numals the evil eye and was clearly uneasy in their presence. When the drinks arrived I settled back and introduced my crew.

"My name is David, I am the commander of this small mixed fleet. This is Barney, my first officer and this is Charlie, she is in charge of supplies and all things medical. You have already met Lank. May I ask who you are?"

The Numal commander stood and after giving us the once over stated.

"I am fleet commander Starn of the Numal nation this is my scientific officer and this is our chief engineering officer. The other three officers are ship captains. You will no doubt understand that our senior captains are of course, on board their ships in case of any emergency .I got the impression he meant us. There was not a lot I could say.

"How can we help you? We are survivors from varlous attacks and we are trying to find some where to start again. "

I told him how I came to be there and the story of the others. He told us his story. The Uxtomals had attacked his fleet and having overwhelming odds defeated Starns force. Star n retreated and got away but, when the Numals tried to return to their home world they found themselves being attacked again and again. When they failed to raise any response by radio they could only conclude that their home world had fallen to the enemy Reduced by this time to twenty two ships from a fleet of two hundred, Starn and his crew decided to find another planet to live on.

till they were strong enough to beat the Uxtomals. It was while this search was going on that they ran into the Xiobargs. The Numals had lost twelve of their ships before the last Xiobarg ship was destroyed, It was with extreme caution that they had approached Lanks ship, after the reception they got from the Xiobargs. I asked again how we could help.?

"We are basically a peaceful race, quite frankly what happen ed with the Xiobargs and Uxtomals has totally thrown us. We only built a large fleet hoping to frighten the Uxtomals away without fighting. We are not really soldiers or explorers. We have been following you for days before we contacted you and we would like to join with you if you will let us. We would be willing to share our knowledge with you in return. "

"As I said before, commander Starn, we also are fleeing from the Xiobargs. You are willing to share your knowledge, would you be willing to share your ships? By that I mean to integrate your people with ours .What I want is your technical expertise in return for our military know how." I then said.

"What do you say to that for starters?"

He looked at his officers then asked if they could consult in private This I agreed to as I wanted to talk to my own people as well. We had an answer within two hours. Starn told me, on behalf of his people, that they agreed to our terms. This was great news! I had convinced my lot that this was a good idea, Charlie was the last to agree, and only then after I had threatend to put her in a shuttle and tow her behind the fleet. We discussed our plans but it was agreed that transfer of craw members wouldn't start till we had found a planet on which to land. The Numal scanners were far superior to anything we had so one of their ships acted as rear guard. In this way we travelled for weeks without

incident. He also had a Numal ship on point and it was this ship that informed us of a planet ahead of us that was capable of supporting our life forms. We chose a large flat plain with a river running through it and after we landed I made sure that a fence was put up in case of animal attacks.

This world looked quiet enough but you never could tell. One ship was in space as a look out and as an early warning system. while the main part of both crews started to make our base habitable. The Numal leaders headed by Starn and Charlie, Barney and myself, sat down to work out the finer points of our alliance. By the end of the third day we had finished our talks and as everyone still lived on board the ships we decided to tell them our decisions after the evening meal. The main points were, I would be in overall command of the combined fleet. Starn and Barney would be my lieutenants and Charlie would command the medical corp. Bran was in charge of ground forces. A special force of scientific staff would be formed with two branches. One would be the development of weapons, the other the peaceful side of medicines and food production. Everyone seemed happy with these proposals. I was having one of the Numal ships as my flag ship so I had Com moved over and began settling into my new quarters. I was talking to the head of weapons development, the Prof, and I mentioned that I thought it was remarkable that the different people could do so many jobs, especially the female Bloorans. They seemed to be able to operate the Numal machinery without any bother. I was surprised when he told me of the Numal teaching machine. He took me to a part of the ship I hadn't visited and showed me the device. He told me to sit in a chair and asked me what subject 1 would like to learn. I thought and then said I would like to learn to speak the Numal, language and as an after thought and Blooran as I was fed up with carrying a voice translator about. He selected a couple of discs about the size of a compact disc, put a pair of headphones on me, told me to sit back and relax then pressed a couple of buttons and smiled.

"Once more, well what do you think of that?"

I felt disappointed, I hadn't felt a thing.

"I don't think it worked Prof, I didn't feel or hear anything. "

"Give me the box, now then any change?"

As I watched him put the box down on a bench I replied that no I still didn't feel any different. He asked me if I was sure and as I was about to reply I realised that I understood him without the box. This was great! I asked if any subject could be taught and how did the machine work. He told me that the device worked by implanting the knowledge into the subconcious mind and anything could be learned in this way. Also the machine could, by the same method, extract knowledge onto a disc. Both methods were painless. Over the next two weeks I was a regular visiter to the machine and I implanted a least to disc's a session.

BOOK – 2

We had been on the planet a year, and things were going fine. We had in that time, explored every inch of our new world, We had also set up a military training camp as well as building a space port and Charlie had organised the building of the hospital and seemed very happy. I think this was a result of all the injuries caused by the training and building accidents. Most of the females had joined her staff so it was quite large. The Numals fitted right in and the most amazing were the scientists. The stuff they came up with was unbelievable, the Prof and his team had invented a new weapon. It was a cannon"cum"energy disperser. Apparently when fired at the enemy ship, it would nullify his defence screens, leaving him open to attack. The Prof and his gang were understandably happy with themselves till I asked about our own screens. They'd forgotten about the fact that we had to fire through our own screens first! Mumbling something about petty little things they retired back to their workshop. We had made sure everyone had a shot of the longevity serum and everything looked to be ok. Barney had married a Blooran girl who I nicknamed Betty, (I was of course the only one to see the joke) and Lank spent most of his time with a young Cammeel girl. Charlie was at the hospital most of the time and I had a sneaky feeling that she also was seeing someone. Time began to drag, with virtually nothing for me to do and nobody to talk too I was bored! I began to pester the scientists and I had used every disc in the learning machine, even ones on the poetry of the Numals! I racked my brain for something, anything, to do, Then I had it, I would mount a campaign against the Xiobarges I authorised the requisition of stores for four ships,

82

two Numal and two of our own. We had the usual scout ships on board, we also had fully stocked science labs and workshops, as well as hospital facility. Besides the usual compliment each ship would also carry a team of scientists and our newly formed ground attack force. It took us two months to get ready. Charlie had wanted to come along but I wouldn't let her, I put Starn in charge of the land base with orders to set up a defence network as soon as possible. Lank I left in charge of the remaining ships and I took Barney as commander of the second Numal ship. The Prof had flatly refused to remain behind so he was in charge of the scientists with instructions to perfect his new weapon before we met any enemies. We had been travelling for two weeks, testing our new systems and weapons when our advance scout reported a sighting. It turned out to be an Xiobarg advance outpost. Leaving a ship on lookout I ordered my ships to attack. We first nutralised the defence screen then just plastered them with lasers before sending in the ground force. I landed with my troops and then followed them in, We killed every one of the Xiobargs, even their wounded. We suffered one casualty, an over excited Numal who entered a building without throwing in a grenade first. There were over a thousand dead Xiobargs! We took any thing which could prove useful and destroyed the rest. After we reembarked we set of deeper into enemy held space. It wasn't very long before our sensors detected, at extreme range, a fleet of nine ships. It took us two days to catch up to them. Before they knew what was happening we had destroyed the three escorts and surrounded the freighters.We jammed any transmissions and told the Xiobargs to abandon their ships or face certain death. As shuttle after shuttle left the freighters I contacted the Xiobarg leader, after he had confirmed that all his men had left we blew them away. Never leave a live enemy, this was the rule we lived by now The boarding party sent across found spares and stores on the first four freighters and information regarding the location of a ground base. The other two ships contained prisoners! This was good news! Some of them were aliens none of us had seen before and some were aliens I knew all too well, Uxtomals| We set up a court room and the Uxtomals were tried for crimes against free worlds and their peoples. We found them guilty and the sentence was death. This was carried out in the main hanger where they were shot and their bodies cast into space. Some of the released prisoners were all right and elected to stay aboard but the badly injured were put back on the freighters and under the command of a junior officer I sent them back to Home World. After the freighters had left I ordered our ships to head for the Xiobarg base. Our journey was uneventful and we located the base easily enough. Our strategy was the same used on the first base and before long this one was destroyed as well, this time with no loss of life on our side. We sailed along for another two weeks and found absolutely nothing. We hadn't been wasting our time though, we had made star charts and transmitted the information regarding the planets we had attacked back to home world. You never knew, we might want to use them at a later date. I'd had enough. What with the look on Barneys face and the fact we had found nothing else I decided it was time to return home. I ordered full speed and we reached home a week later and five hours behind the freighters! The rescued prisoners had all been taken to the hospital and were being well looked after, the stores were still being unloaded.

I promoted the officer who was in charge of the freighters and declared shore leave for all hands. We had a big celebration to mark our victories I got smashed and made a complete arse of myself I don't think I did Earth's reputation a lot of good but what the hell! We got a call, a week later, from our cruiser stationed on lookout.He was picking up deep apace transmissions. I got the captain to patch them through to us and after Com had decoded and translated them we found we were onto something big, They were Xiobarg in origin, It seemed they were at a loss as to what or who had destroyed their bases. They were sending a fleet of ships fifteen in total, to seek out and destroy whoever was responsible.

This was a chance to try out our new weapons in actual battle conditions If they didn't work we wouldn't be able to complain The Xiobargs knew only that the Uxtomals were not the attackers, and they even gave us the location of their rendezvous, I decided to take six ships this time, it was a big chunk of our fleet, but I felt that the risk was worth taking. We had two weeks to reach the rendezvous, after that it would be a search and find mission.We arrived not long after the Xiobargs. We had been monitoring their signals for two days. I didn't want the enemy to get settled so I orderded full speed and we attacked without warning. There were five big ships and ten cruisers, three of their cruisers were destroyed almost immediately. After the initial surprise, the battle took on a more tactical aspect. As well as developing our new weapons the Prof and his team had also increased our defence screen efficiency. This soon began to tell and one by one the enemy ships were knocked out. True to form the Xiobargs fought till the very end. Only one of our ships suffered any real damage, this was caused by a lucky hit as they opened a hole in their screen to fire through. We had destroyed or crippled fifteen enemy ships for the loss of fourteen dead and twenty three serious wounded. The damage to our ship was under repair and would take about three hours. I called the ships captains and we held a conference. Every ship had suffered minor damage and injured crew, from minor cuts to broken bones. The main topic on the agenda was the base on the nearby planet. It was decided to attack after a scout ship had checked out the base. The captain of the scout was immediately shown into the meeting room on his return. His report made us rethink our attack plan. This base wasn't the same as the others we had destroyed. This one had prisoners in the main compound! The enemy forces were assessed at twenty thousand plus! We had a total of fifteen hundred ground troops! Everyone was waiting for me to speak.

At first I thought of trying to draw the Xiobargs out of their prepared positions and into the open were our fighters could get at them. The only problem with this idea was the Xiobargs. I didn't think they would be stupid enough to leave a well prepared defensive position. At the moment they were in the better position, they could afford to wait, we couldn't! We were, of course, jamming their signals but eventually Xiobarg ships would come to investigate. I ordered scouts to be positioned around the base while we could think of a way to extract the prisoners without getting our ground forces wiped out.

We thought of infiltrating the base and knocking out the automatic defence system. This seemed like a good idea till I pointed out that the Xiobargs would probably kill all the prisoners in retaliation. The Prof then suggested we use a germ bomb. We all stopped and stared at him. He went on to explain. He and his team had been working on a virus derived from the flu germ that I had infected everyone with before. He believed that we could drop a bomb into the base that would infect all the Xiobargs and of course the prisoners within a week. When I asked him how long it would take to make the bomb he said it was ready now.

Brilliant ! We got mowing. A fighter was fitted with two bombs and then launched. We informed our scouts on the ground and sat back to wait.

We waited a week before the effects started to show. One of our scouts, a non com, had been in and out of the compound on a regular basis all week. He was the one who informed us of the state of the Xiobargs. He shut down the automated defences. He warned the friendly prisoners to keep their heads down in case of fighting. After the base was secure we transported all the friendly prisoners to our ships. The Xiobargs and Uxtomal prisoners were tried and executed. After we had destroyed the Xiobarg base, we decided to return to our home world. We had captured four enemy ships and blown up eleven more plus one large enemy base. We were quite pleased with ourselves and besides, the released prisoners needed medical care and attention that they couldn't get on board our ships. When we had got under way, I called the commander of our ground troops and asked him to send the non com who had done such good work in the attack to see me. I had the other ships captains brought over and we discussed our tactics during the battle with the enemy fleet and the base. While we were thus engaged, I was informed that the non com had arrived. I had him shown in. The look of surprise on his face was quickly masked as he came to attention and saluted. At first I was wondering who he was saluting, then it dawned on me, he was saluting me! It still makes me wonder how I came to be in charge of this mix of aliens. Recovering quickly I saluted him back.

"What is your name ?"

"Brom, 1st attack company sir. "

"Forget the sir bit Brom and sit down. "

I don't think I ever will get used to being called sir.

"From what your commanding officer said, you were in and out of the Xiobarg base from day one. Is that correct?"

"Yes sir. "

"When I spoke to your commander he told me that he had given orders that no one was to put themselves at risk, they were to watch and report, nothing else. Is that correct?"

"Yes sir.

"So you disobeyed a direct order, is that correct?"

"Well er, " He was puzzled with my questioning.

"Is that correct! "

He was getting flustered, I had started to pace up and down.

"It seems to me there is only one thing to do, I am taking your stripes away and removing you from the attack force. "

His face now registered shock!

"But sir. "

"Shut up. What you will be doing from now on Brom is," I paused for what to him must have seemed like hours. "Starting a special force to do exactly what you did at the Xiobarg base. It will be comprised of a small but highly trained team of men, led by you and based upon soldiers from my planet. I will inform the attack commander that you have the authority to recruit, say thirty men. This should be enough to start with. I will see you later to discuss tactics, You may leave now leiutenant".

He sat there stunned, then a smile spread across his face. He jumped up saluted said yes sir and then fairly flew out of the room. The others were as astonished as Bron had been till I explained that we would undoubtably come up against more enemy bases in the future. What we all needed were more ships.We had made a move to stop the Xiobargs conquest of space but without ships we would lose in a war of attrition. We could of course convert enemy ships but the way that they fought we would only get the odd one or two and they would only be cruisers. The mother ships out gunned us. We tried to think of ways but in the end we put the problem in the hands of the scientists. The Prof and his boys worked like devils. We had been back on our home world about three months, and I was getting restless. Bron had set his training camp up about five miles away in the foothills of our local mountain, I had told him of the S. A. S and other crack teams of highly skilled soldiers of Earth and he had been very impressed. When I asked him if his men were ready he said they couldn't wait to get at the enemy whoever they were. This was what I had been hoping for. I ordered him to embark his men on to my ship with enough ammo and explosives to destroy half the solar system! Then I called all the top commanders to a meeting to tell them what I wanted to do. When they were all seated I outlined my plan. I told them I was going on a extended foray against the Xiobargs, and that I would be gone at least six months maybe more, depending on what found. I put Starn in command of home, world, Barney would command the ships left behind and Lank would accompany me as my second in command Charlie jumped up before I could say anything and stated that she was coming too and that was an end to it. Well what could I say, I put her in charge of food and medical supplies. We set out three days later.

While we cruised onward, we checked the bases we had already attacked. Only one of them was being rebuilt. We scanned for prisoners and as there wasn't any we plastered the place. After this we cruised for a couple of days. I was starting to think the Xiobargs had all changed galaxies when I was informed that our long range communication scanners were picking up Xiobarg messages. After they had been decoded and translated we were enraged to find out that tho Xiobargs had been ordered to exterminate all prisoners if they were attacked! This made Bron and his men indispensable. I told Bron that he must intensify his infiltration technique training from now on as his team would be used more and more. We tracked the messages and found them to have passed between a ground base and a fleet of Xiobarg ships that were two days cruising from us. I ordered Bron and his men onto one of our cruisers with orders to attack the ground base while the rest of our ships would go for the enemy fleet. While we chased the enemy, I had a

meeting with the Prof and his team of boffins. They had invented a weapon, "THE DEATH RAY"as the Prof called it, that would dissolve the flesh of it's intended victim before their very eyes, while they were still alive! All we had to do was knock out the enemy shields, punch a few holes in the ship and then close to about a thousand yards before the actual firing of the ray took place! When I pointed out that the enemy would be firing back with the intention of destroying us the Prof said this was incidental. Incidental! The Prof and his team were discussing the new ray as though it was a toy, I was going to have something to eat but the way they talked about the rays effect on flesh put me right off. As mine was the only ship to be fitted so far with the "DEATH RAY" we would be in the front line. I asked the Prof if he and his team could not come up with a weapon that could be fired from a greater distance with the same effect. No was tho emphatic reply but they had nearly completed work on a new torpedo. This would, apparently, pass through a defence screen and explode between the screen and the ship blinding all its sensors. In theory!

I asked him to work as fast as he could. The look he gave me! I was informed that science was not to be rushed. With that parting remark, he and his team departed. After two more days we came up to the enemy fleet. It was bigger than I had anticipated. We had two mother ships and three cruisers while the Xiobargs had four mother ships and fifteen cruisers. They also had ten freighters with them. They had spotted us by this time and were deploying their ships accordingly. I did the only thing possible under the circumstances. I orderded them to surrender. The Xiobarg leader laughed at me, at least that's what I thought he did. It's not a pretty sight, an Xiobarg laughing. Outnumbering us as they did he must of thought it was funny, We attacked. He didn't laugh long! With our stronger shields it wasn't long before we were knocking out the enemy ships. We had tried the Profs new weapon but till we could actually board one of the enemy ships we couldn't tell what effect it was really having. I did recieve a message from the Prof asking if we could stop throwing the ship around to much as he was trying to work. We had reduced the enemy fleet by half for the loss of one of our cruisers when the Xiobarg commander ordered the freighters to make a run for it. This we had to stop, we had been jamming their signals so a warning or request for help would not get out, but if the freighters got away they would raise the alarm. I deployed one of our cruisers to head them off. We could tell by the frantic inter ship signals that the Xiobargs were getting pretty worried. They couldn't understand how an inferior force was defeating them. We lost another cruiser. They were finally learning. They ganged up on him, his shields overloaded and bang, Gone. The enemy was down to one mothership and three cruisers, it was too late for them to make any use of the knowledge they had gained. Even if they had wanted to surrender, it was too late. It wans't long before we had destroyed the last of their fighting ships, then we turned our attention to the freighters. I called to the senior officer on board to surrender. This he did without any delay. When I asked if he had any prisoners onboard he replied in the affirmative. I told him to board their shuttle craft and to leave the freighters without harming the captives. When all the Xiobargs had left and were a safe distance from the freighters I ordered one of the cruisers to destroy then. I sent some of our crews aboard the freighters with instructions to dispose of any Uxtomals and to see to the welfare of the others. They would then fly the ships back to our home world. I also sent a cruiser back to see how Bron was getting on. While all this was going on Lank had taken a boarding party across to the Xiobarg ships that we had tried the new ray on. His report was better than I had expected The four ships that remained were in good condition but would require extensive cleaning! The look on his face said it all, the new ray was effective but messy. We took the ships in tow and followed the ship I had sent to Bron. We had not come out of the fight without damage and some casualties but It wouldn't take long to repair and Charlie and her team were in action on the injured. Before we reached the Xiobarg ground base one of our cruisers rejoined us and told us that Bron and his team were still in the process of infiltrating the defences. Apparently there were some captives, the majority of which were Uxtomals. Bron was trying to separate them from our people. The intention was of getting our people out of the prisoner compound then blowing the rest up.

A good plan. It would save time. Unfortunately it didn't work out that way. While in the process of removing our kind from the others Bron was discovered, the Xiobargs killed them all. when this was reported I ordered all remaining ground forces to be withdrawn and when this had been successfully completed we totally destroyed the base. I mean totally, We mourned the loss of Bron who had been a brave and resourceful commander but life must go on. We reached home world without further incident. The freighters had yielded a lot of much needed supplies, raw materials and some heavy machinery which we put to good use. Our forays were getting further and further away from home world till it was taking us four months just to get back home! On the next foray, we had been out for about seven months before we got any contact with the Xiobargs. It turned out to be a small ground base. As we approached it we picked up a signal between the base and an incoming unknown number of Xiobarg ships. I ordered one of my cruisers to attack the base while the rest of our ships would go for the enemy ships. When we came in range we found that there were only six cruisers and ten freighters in the fleet. We heavily outnumbered them with our four mother ships and five cruisers, we also had our superior shields and the death ray. We had been jamming any signals they had been trying to make and it wasn't long before we had either

destroyed or crippled their ships. The freighters carried the usual cargo of prisoners and supplies. The Xiobargs were given the usual treatment and after we had boarded the freighters, the Uxtomal prisoners were shown a like courtesy. I decided to return to the planet with the base on it and to see how our cruiser had got on.

Imagine my surprise when I found out that the captain of our ship instead of destroying the base, had captured it. I had him brought aboard my ship and asked him what he thought he was doing by disobeying a direct order. "Well captain Brad, explain yourself." He was standing to attention with that look on his face that says I'm right and I don't care what you think! He composed himself then said.

"I didn't destroy the base sir because I thought we could use it ourselves. Now that we are expanding we will need forward bases such as this. "

He paused there with a look at me, begging me to understand his motives. I stared back at him for a couple of minutes, just long enough for him to start feeling uncomfortable before asking about any Xiobarg prisoners. His attitude had changed in those few minutes and his reply was a bit more subdued.

"I executed the Xiobargs as per standing orders sir, but the Uxtomal prisoners are under guard in the compound. I thought that we could use them for labour like they used our people. "

His voice trailed off and I let him stand there for about five minutes while I just stared at him with no expression on my face what so ever. He was getting more and more nervous with each passing second and when I spoke he nearly jumped out of his skin!

"Well done Brad, I was thinking about the very same thing. We could really use another base and as our people can't work and fight at the same time we will need someone to do the work. Yes an excellent idea. How long will it be before we can use the base?"

"The base is intact sir although the defences don't work, which is probably why the Xiobargs didn't last long, It shouldn't take long to get them working. There is also a very large flat area just outside the compound that will make an excellent, space port. "

"Well Brad I'm going to leave you in charge of the place. We captured ten freighters and all their stores. You can have the lot and I will also leave you all our cruisers as a defence against attack. Leave one on station at least two days out to give advanced warning and if any fleet bigger than yours approaches return to home world as quick as you can after destroying the base and of course the Uxtomals. Is all that clear ?" After he had left with a huge grin on his face I asked the Prof to see me. I wanted to leave Brad with the best possible chance of success. We stayed for about three months then departed for home world. I left behind a very happy Brad, The prof and his team had installed defence screens similar to those on board our ships and also some of the ray guns around the compound and also on board the cruisers. Brad and his men were as safe as we could possibly make them. I had promised Brad that we would return as soon as possible, I was still worried though. It was a feeling akin to leaving your child for the first time with a baby sitter. We reached home world without incident and turned over the captured ships to the work shops. While these ships were repaired and converted our injured were seen to. My original ships were repaired and restocked ready to leave on another foray into enemy space. It took six months! Six months of sitting on my backside signing paper! I was going out of my mind getting fat and generally, getting on peoples nerves with my constant irritability. Finally everything was ready, and as the engines were warming up I opened a channel to all vessels and said "Lets rock and roll people." You think I would have learned by now, It's not my fault if aliens don't have a sense of humour. With the death of Bron the "commandoes" had been absorbed back into the general ground forces We would need them again so I had promoted Bron's second in command and instructed him to reform his unit. When we set off on our latest foray, we had taken a different direction from our previous ones. We would travel in a wide circle and call in on Brad as we returned to home world. As usual I had a cruiser out in front and for two weeks we had no sight or sound of the enemy. As we approached a group of planets we picked up signals, a ground base! The signals were being sent to an enemy fleet, they were asking for supplies. As we had not been in this part of space before we were hoping to surprise the Xiobargs. I sent a cruiser with Blor's team on board to attack the ground base while we set out to find the enemy fleet. As we travelled in the direction that the signals had been sent the Prof came to see me.

"Well Prof, what have you and your team invented now? Is it a new type of ray that turns its victims inside out or some equally gory result?"

He just stared at me with a pitying look in his eyes, shook his head, then said.

"No it isn't. What we have discovered though is probably just as effective as a weapon. we have invented a machine that will make our ships invisible to the enemy. "

He said it so matter of factly that it didn't register straight away

"What?"

He sighed, gave me another of those pitying looks then explained the theory of light refraction. It was as clear as mud to me. Apparently these machines threw a screen around the ship that stopped the penetration of sensor beams and deflected them. The prof and his team had also devised a counter against this so that we could pick up our own ships. As he said , we didn't want to ram our own ships by accident. They would be installed within three days. Great ! Unfortunately the Xiobargs didn't give us that time. The next day our scout reported a large fleet of enemy ships approaching, There were six mother ships an twenty cruisers plus thirty freighters! We had four mother ships and five cruisers not counting the cruiser attacking the ground base. I was about to have a message sent to this cruiser telling them to abort the mission when we received one from them. It wasn't good news They had landed Blor and his team when they had been attacked by two Xiobarg cruisers that must have been on the planet. The fight was still going on. They requested help as they couldn't pick up Blor's team till the enemy cruisers were disposed of. What to do? If I sent help to Blo'rs team I would be wakening my own force. The Xiobarg fleet had detected us by this time so to pull back to the ground base would only add to Blor's problem as we still wouldn't be able to pick him up. I could leave them to their fate. I did the only thing I could do! I attacked which took the Xiobargs by surprise, they had expected us to run, outnumbering us as they did. We had knocked out three of their cruisers before they retaliated. The battle raged for days! When we had first attacked we had formed a V formation with the mother ships in the van. Their mother ships were in the rear. with our superior shields and the ray as well as our conventional weapons we had a far better chance even though they out numbered us. Another thing on our side was the fact that not all their ships could attack us at the same time. At the end of the third day we had won the field. A few of the enemy cruisers had escaped but the rest were either damaged or destroyed. Our own losses were one mother ship and four out of five cruisers. One of the remaining mother ships had to be blown up later as the damage it had suffered was too great to repair. The Xiobarg freighters had skirted the battle and gone down on to the ground base. We couldn't take any of the enemy ships back with us so we had to destroy them as well. Sorting out the surviving crews from our damaged ships we set course for the ground base, I didn't expect anything but more bad news when we arrived. Our cruiser had destroyed the enemy cruisers but had been unable to prevent the freighters from landing. These had landed thousands of Xiobarg ground troops who were attacking our forces in the ground base! The cruiser had been unable to help as it had suffered severe engine damage.They only had sufficient power for the life support systems. I sent our other mother ship to attack the Xiobargs. They wiped out the troops and freighters then picked up our own ground forces. I had Blor brought to me and he made his report.

He had landed with thirty men, they had only taken pistols with them. They then had mingled with the prisoner work parties and been taken into the compound. For three days they had suffered with the prisoners until their chance had come. They had killed their guards and with the help of the released prisoners had attacked and taken over the base They knew the cruiser was under attack and after the Xiobarg freighters had landed they had repeatedly repulsed every enemy attack. He made it sound so easy and matter of fact. Of his original team of thirty only eight survived, six were wounded, two critically. We were well on our way back to home world. There were only three ships left of our original ten, two mother ships and one cruiser. The other cruiser had to be blown up as it was impossible to repair her engines. We had won the battle but at what a high price. There wasn't a crew member without some sort of injury. I myself had a broken arm and various cuts and bruises. I had Blor and his remaining men promoted and instructed them to set up a fifty man team each with Blor in overall command.

The prof perfected his invisibility machines and installed them. He would fit them to all our ships once we reached home world. They would be a big asset in our fight against the

Xiobargs. The longevity drug helped everyone to get over their injuries quickly but it couldn't help if you were vaporised. We could always get more ships but we couldn't replace the experienced crews as quickly. The next two years passed without any real untoward incident happening. We made a few forays into Xiobarg space, knocking off the odd cruiser or freighter and adding them to our fleet. The invisibility machine worked perfectly. The Xiobargs were dead before they even knew we were there! We'd sneak up, knock a hole or two in the hull of their ship then fire our death ray and a new addition to our fleet! The prof and his team did come up with a new weapon but it was more of a danger to us than the enemy! It had the power to vaporise a mother ship with one shot! That was the trouble, you only got the one shot! The weapon so drained your ships power that when we tried it, we had to tow our test ship home! During this period I had another shock. I had been organising a raiding party when Charlie came to see me. Before she could say anything I said she could come with us, she looked a little sheepish then said she didn't want to come along! I couldn't believe it! Charlie not wanting to go on an expedition was totally unexpected! The reason was another shock. She wanted to get married! You could have knocked me down with a feather. I stared at her with my mouth open like an idiot. It turned out that the last bunch of prisoners had among them a man that Charlie had known for a long time, she had thought him dead when the Xiobargs had overrun her world, She had been spending a lot of time with him while he had been recovering from his injuries. What could I say but congratulations It seemed that everyone was getting married but me. We set off the next day, travelling ever deeper into Xiobarg occupied space. My fleet was made up of six mother ships and six of the captured freighters. We had the freighters fitted with the new weapons and their screens were stronger.

With the cloaking device they were a match for any enemy cruiser. What I most wanted to find were enemy bases, hopefully with lots of prisoners to rescue. With this in mind I had Blor and his team along. There had not been a name for Blors men before so while we were cruising I asked him if he had thought of one.

"The only thing I can think of is soaks, sir."

"Soaks? Is that an abbreviation?"

"Yes sir, it means Seek Out And Kill. "

"I see, Your happy with that, You don't want to change it do you?"

I was smiling as I said it, thinking that a soak on Earth is a drunk!

"Yes sir quite happy. "

He gave me a puzzled look. I told him we would have to make up a company badge for his men and suggested, a ship above a planet with the initials below. He seemed happy with that and he went off to organise the making of them. The next few day passed uneventfully.

I had ordered all our ships to use the cloaking device as we were in unfamiliar space. We eventually came upon a planet with a base but when we scanned it we found it to be deserted. We travelled on the next base we found was also deserted! What was going on? I could not believe that we had caused the Xiobargs to pull out. I didn't think our attacks had been damaging enough, or that the Xiobargs suddenly turned into cowards, We travelled on. About a week later our scanners pick ed up five blips. I decided to shadow them. We followed them for four days, then we detected six more ships. The new ships joined the original five and carried on. They were all cruisers. I would have liked to attack and capture them but I wanted to know what was going on. We followed. More ships joined them till there were twenty in total, seventeen cruisers and three freighters. Com picked up a transmission from the Xiobargs and after translation I read it. It came as a shock. The Xiobargs had been developing new weapons as well! They were calling in their ships to have them fitted with them. This was because of a new alien threat. They must mean us! I made an instant decision. I ordered all ships to attack. These ships wouldn't be fitted with new weapons. With our cloaking devices on the Xiobargs didn't stand a chance. The cruisers lasted about five minutes. We were blocking their transmissions so no word got out. As the last cruiser was destroyed I called the freighters and told them to surrender. I also ordered my ships to turn of the cloaking devices. The Xiobargs must have nearly popped out of their skins when so many enemy ships appeared as if from nowhere. They climbed aboard their shuttles and departed. They didn't, of course, get far. The freighters only carried supplies, these would come in very handy in deed. I decided to return via our forward base. I would warn Brad and leave the supplies with him. We didn't meet any opposition and arrived at the base without incident. Brad was pleased to see us and was grateful for the supplies, I brought him up to date with the Xiobargs. His defences had been upgraded and he seemed confident that he and his men could hold out if attacked. I was a little worried, I would not settle till I found out what the new Xiobarg weapons were. A week later we set off for home world. We had only been home a couple of days when we received a message from Brad. He was under attack from a large force of Xiobargs. I ordered an immediate provisioning of all available ships. It took a full day before we were ready to sail. I couldn't take our full force as it would mean leaving home world undefended. I decided that four mother ships and ten cruisers would be enough. we put on maximum speed as soon as possible. We were still two days away from the base when we met one of the cruisers that we had left there. We had, for some time, been travelling with our cloaking devices on, The captain called our ship and we turned off the device. I ordered the captain aboard my ship, I also had the other captains brought aboard. The captain from the base didn't pull any punches. All our ships but his had been destroyed and the base had been completely wiped out ! Our ships had used the cloaking device when the Xiobargs had first been detected. They had sailed to meet the Xiobarg fleet which was made up of mother ships and cruisers, no freighters. They numbered five hundred! Our ships totalled three cruisers and six freighters. The freighters had stayed behind to act as a screen whilst the three cruisers had attacked. They had all used the cloaking device and had hoped to surprise the enemy by getting amongst them before opening fire. This had worked for a couple of hours with twelve of the enemy ships being destroyed or crippled. The Xiobargs had even fired on their own ships! Suddenly, the Xiobargs had changed tactics. They had fired what looked like harmless shells randomly. When these shells burst they had emitted a blinding white light. Our captain told us that he and the other captains had been bewildered by this action till the enemy then started to pour concentrated fire straight at our ships.

He said it was as though the enemy could see them! When he had reported this to Brad, he had ordered him to return to home world with the news The other cruisers and then the freighters were destroyed. when he would have stayed to fight, Brad had again ordered him to speed straight to us. He had tried to keep in touch with the base but after a short time communications had failed. The prof had been listening to all this quietly. I asked him for his opinion. He said the only thing he could think of was that the shells, on exploding, emitted some sort of ray that showed our ships to the Xiobarg sensors making it easier for their weapons to lock onto our ships. We carried on to the base. I wasn't very hopeful of finding any one alive but we had to see. When we arrived it was to find nothing but a smoking ruin. I had troops landed and they searched the wreckage. There were no one left alive. The Xiobargs had total ly annihilated the place. From the evidence found they had bombed the hell out of the place then sent in their ground troops to finish anyone left alive. They hadn't just shot the survivors, they had mutilated and tortured them first. It was a sickening sight. We had not only lost lot of men but eight ships we couldn't replace. The base was totally useless to us as well. This was our first defeat since we had joined forces to hit back at the Xiobargs. So many good men gone! The cruiser I had sent as a lookout was sent to find the enemy fleet. I ordered them to stay at extreme sensor range and under no circumstances were they to engage the enemy. Every ship was precious. I consulted the Prof. We had to find a solution to the Xiobarg weapons and we had to find it fast! It took us over a week to locate the Xiobarg fleet. I had been with the Prof for most of that time discussing various weapons, both of attack and of defence. I had told him about the mines developed on Earth and had asked him for longer ranged weapons. We had talked about guns and missiles and he had been deep in thought with his team. One of the weapons they had come up with was a mine. I laughed when I saw it, it was about three inches by two. When challenged about its power the prof asked me what I knew about science. I had to admit very little, He then went into a lecture about varioos compounds and chemicals. In other words he was telling me to shut up about something I knew nothing about. We had nothing to try it out on so I thought I was justified in being sceptical. When we picked up the enemy fleet he got his chance to show me what the new mine could do. I sent a cruiser in a wide arc and far out of the enemy sensor range with orders to sow a field of mines in their path. It took our ship a couple of days to do this. Luckily the Xiobargs didn't seem to be in any rush. The Prof and his boys had only produced about a hundred of the mines so they were spread pretty thinly. our ship did its job and got out of the area. We sat back to watch. We knew roughly the position of the minefield but we couldn't pick up the actual mines because they were too small. The explosion, when it came, far exceeded my expectations. To say it was spectacular is an understatement! An Xiobarg cruiser was in the van of their fleet, this ship hit one of the mines. The explosion blew it into another one and when the dust had settled there wasn't enough left for our sensors to pick up! The rest of the enemy fleet was in a state of panic.Star shells were going of all over the place. We were well out of range. The signals from the enemy were full of confusion, not knowing what had happened with no visible enemy they were really up tight. It was some time before their commander restored order and ordered his ships forward. I would have liked to know where they were going but when another ship hit a mine and had its self blown in half the commander decided to pull back and rethink the situation. I decided that we would attack them. A hit and run tactic seemed best. I had my ships line up and we shot forward. I had told the other captains what I wanted to do. We would concentrate on the cruisers as it took a lot more shots to put a mother chip out of action let alone blow one up. I had told my cruiser captains to double up on one enemy cruiser, the mother ships would of course attack an enemy cruiser alone. This was because the enemy would have their defence screens up. I had one cruiser over, the one from the forward base. I told the captain to hang

104

back on this occasion as he and his men had already been in battle. It wasn't till later that I found out he had disobeyed my orders, Our attack worked well, we destroyed nine

enemy ships. We also lost one, the one from the forward base. The ship attacked an enemy cruiser but when the rest of us retreated they pressed their attack. The Xiobargs fired their star shells but only picked up one enemy ship. Their massed fire power destroyed our cruiser in seconds. The Xiobarges continued to fire all around them for sometime. We were well out of range. Suddenly we picked up a message directed at us!

"We know you are out there, show your selves and we will kill you quickly. You cannot escape us, we are all powerful."

I got Com to open a communication link with the enemy ship that was sending out the signal. The Xiobarg looked surprised when I appeared on his screens. This soon changed to one of total surprise when I spoke.

"Hi shit for brains, how ya doing?"

"I have newer seen an alien like you before, who are you?"

"I'm the boy who is going to kick your ass out of the galaxy, dogs breath."

"I am an Xiobarg, I have newer seen a dogs breath or heard of a planet of that name. Why have you attack my ships?"

"You are some brassed necked, bare faced motherless cretin to ask a question like that arn't you."

"I do not understand you." How can you insult someone when they haven't the faintest idea what sarcansm, wit and a sense of humour are. Aliens are no fun!

"Right! I am an Earthman, my shipmates are Bloorans Cammeels and Numals plus a few other races. Does that answer your questions?"

"I have newer heard of any place called Earth. The other races you mentioned have all been destroyed by the glorious Xiobarg war fleets and enslaved. When we capture you, Earthman, I will put you on display as a novelty for our children to laugh at."

"It's been nice talking to you but you are obviously mentally disturbed so I will give you a chance. If you surrender now I will let you take a shuttle and go. But you only have five minuets to make up your mind then we will attack you and destroy your whole fleet. ok". To say he was amazed at this offer would be an understatement. It was a couple of minuets before he answered.

"You cannot defeat us, the races you mentioned do not have the resources left to fight with. we vastly out number you, you are bluffing. Where is this superior fleet, I do not see it. "

"Oh were all around you, You have already lost ships and your'e going to lose a lot more. Well, whilst we have been chatting, your time has run out .Now we are going to kick your butts. Bye bye."

As the communication link was cut the Prof appeared and informed me that he had another one hundred or so of the mines ready. This gave me an idea. I had the mines sown in front of us, I ordered my ships to pull back and to shut off the cloaking device. I got the result I wanted. As soon as the Xiobargs saw us appear on their screens they charged at us. We of course pulled back. Their lead ships ran right into the mines and five had been destroyed or crippled before they could stop. As soon as they stopped I ordered all cloaking devices back on and we moved to another position. whilst they were still recovering we attacked the nearest cruisers. We destroyed four more.

I got Com to open a link with the Xiobarg commander again.

"Is me. How ya doing. Bummer ain't it eh? Float like a butterfly and sting like a bee, You can't shoot what you can't see. Having a bad day? Wished you'd stayed at home?Want to surrender?"

He was fuming, I thought he was going to bust!

"You will regret this Earthman! I will destroy you and all your kind. You cannot evade me for ever. "

"Tell you what chummy, I'll come and get you. I'll leave this link open then when I blow the shit out of you I can watch it"Live! "

Without breaking the link I ordered my other ships to maintain their positions. Then I ordered my ship forward. One or two of my crew looked a little pale but otherwise looked grim. Without the Xiobargs hearing, I ordered my ship to attack the mothership nearest the flag. We sneaked in and let rip with everything we had. The Xiobarg ship disintegrated. As we got out of there I had a few mines dropped as well. I had been keeping up a running commentary, mixed with insults, for the enemy commander. When his sister ship blew up I said. "Oops, sorry, wrong one. Never mind I will get you next time." When this ship had exploded the others around it had started firing all over the place. A couple of shots had hit us but the screens had absorbed the energy. They had also damaged a couple of their own ships. When we had reached a safe distance, we stopped. I continued to taunt the Xiobarg.

"You don't look well commander. You have gone from red to pink. would you like to see us?" Here we are, come and get us. we disengaged the cloaking device. The Xiobarg commander ordered four of his cruisers to attack us. They came a lot slower than before. Even so two were knocked out by the mines. The rest of them stayed were they where. We played with them for days, we knew we could keep it up for ever. There were too many for us to block all their signals. We did manage to knock out about twenty more cruisers and one mothership hit a couple of mines. My crews were just about at their limit so I ordered a withdrawal. We left plenty of mines about so the Xiobargs wouldn't follow us. Just before we left I told the enemy commander that I wasn't going to talk to him any more and that when he least expected it I would attack his flag ship. He must have been a nervous wreck by the time he realised that we had gone. I ordered by ships to shadow the enemy fleet. We had to make sure that they didn't go near our home world. We kept our cloaking devices on and keeping out of range of the enemy guns, followed them. This also gave us a chance to rest ourselves. After two weeks of us darting in front and sowing mines that the Xiobargs blundered into, the enemy decided to change course. They put full speed on. We followed them and as they were heading away from home world, we let them go. The main reason for this was that even though we had been resting we were still in need of shore leave. I detailed one of the cruisers to make sure that the Xiobargs didn't change their minds and alter course. With three weeks uneventful cruising we were back on home world. We had destroyed ninety enemy ships but all joy in this had been muted due to our own irreplaceable losses. Home world was totally different! It didn't seem two minutes since we had left. New buildings, towns and most surprising, children! I was the only who seemed surprised though The prof tried to explain something about time and space. Apparently, while we had spent a year in space, home world time had sped by, five years' This made me think of Earth. What would it be like if I could ever find it! I had got lots of time, excluding enemies, to find my way back.

For the next year things were peaceful, I'd sent out scouts but there wasn't a sign of the Xiobargs. Even the bases we had previously attacked had not been visited by them. The more time I had the more I thought of Earth. If only I could find it again. With the things I now knew I could help them build weapons to fight off any attack from either the Xiobargs or the Uxtomals. With this thought I decided to mount an expedition. First of I asked for volunteers to man my ship.

I told them that I would only take single men as I didn't know how long I would be gone. The Prof came to see me, he and his team had developed a new weapon, surprise, surprise. It was based on the same chemicals that made up the mines. This was a rocket. It could be fired from any part of the ship as it was guided by the sensors. This thing was packed with enough explosive to completely destroy an Xiobarg mothership. He had also made a bomb for use against a ground base. I decided to wait the extra time it took to have a rocket launcher fitted to my ship. I was glad I had waited! Our scout sent a message saying that they had spotted an Xiobarg fleet heading our way. All our ships were being fitted with the rocket launchers including four new cruisers that had been built by our own factories .When all our ships were fully provisioned we sailed to meet the enemy. I had a total of twenty four ships. Five of which were converted freighters. After a weeks sailing we sighted the enemy fleet. It was massive. There were well over a thousand ships. We identified seven hundred fighting ships and three hundred odd freighters. I detailed our on freighters to attack the Xiobarg transports. While they were getting into position I issued orders to my other ships. We had thousands of mines on each ship, these would be our first method of attack.

Only when the enemy fighting ships were committed would our freighter attack. Whilst our freighters had the fire power of a cruiser the armour wasn't as strong and if a shot did get through their screens. it would finish them. Mind you if a shot from an energy cannon hit us it wouldn't do us any good either! My plan was simple, the mines would be first followed by our new rockets as these were long range. When we had used up these weapons we would close in and use the more conventional ones. With my scout ship I now had twenty five ships in total. They out numbered us over forty to one! With the words" Lets get

cooking" which earned me some funny looks. I ordered the attack to begin. We didn't sow all our mines at once, that would have been silly. We dropped a few hundred in their path then sat back to watch. As expected, the First Xiobarg ships, which were cruisers, flew straight into them. The rest of the enemy fleet stopped. we were, of course, monitoring their signals. The next line of ships started firing their canon with good effect. our mines started to blow up without doing any damage. They had learnt from the last time we met. Their commander transmitted a message to us.

"I know your out there Earthman, this time you will not get away. Your puny efforts to stop us are useless. We will destroy your ships first then your world, What do you say to that. "

This would take some thinking about. I didn't bother to answer him. I would need to rethink my plan. If I could split them up it would make it easier to destroy them, but how? Then I had it! I moved all my ships to a different position then had two of my ships switch off their cloaking devices. We were just within the Xiobarg sensor range. We listened while the enemy commander ordered twenty of his ships to attack. He sent two motherships and eighteen cruisers. My plan was simple, my ships split up with the two decoys drawing the Xiobargs between us. As they passed we fired on them with everything we had got.

We totally destroyed them! Our two decoys activated their cloaking devices and we all took up new positions. The Xiobarg commander had sent a hundred ships to the rescue. when they reached the ambush location they fired their star shells but found nothing. When these ships had reported failure the Xiobarg commander ordered them to rejoin the main fleet with all speed. While all this had been going on I had two of my cruisers sow a mine field behind them. They ran right into it. They lost at least twenty ships before they managed to stop. The Xiobarg commander was going barmy! He ordered the remaining ships to

clear the mines while his perimeter ship fired star shells. He didn't find diddly squat! Before he could get settled I ordered two of my ships to fire rocket. I wanted to see what effect they had. Six were fired, four were destroyed but two got through. Unfortunately they hit the same ship which was a cruiser. The rockets were only eight foot long and a cruiser would cover a football field, One would have vaporised it, two and there wasn't even any vapour! Overkill or what.

"Prof if you weren't a male I would marry you! "

"More Earth humour David?"

"That was beautiful, any more weapons like that?"

"Not yet but were working on some.

I had sent a cruiser to sneak in amongst the enemy fleet with the intention of sowing a few mines. He completed his mission but on the way back his cloaking device failed. They were blown out of the sky. What I wanted was to get the Xiobargs away from their transports so my freighters could have a go. We were still monitoring the Xtobarg channels. I thought I'd try the decoy trick again. As our ships showed themselves I expected the Xiobargs to go charging off after them. I was wrong. Their commander wasn't falling for it a second time. He decided to advance instead. This resulted in a few more of his ships being blown up by_our mines. The loss of our cruiser was avenged. We had now been fighting for two days. The Xiobargs had not advanced one foot in that time but we had not stopped them either. I decided to cover all sides of the enemy fleet and to launch a simultaneous rocket attack. We each fired three rockets, out of fifty seven fired ten got through, ten more kills. we were gradually reducing the odds against us but at this rate it would be months before we could go home. I was racking my brain for a winning formula. The only thing I hadn't done was to taunt the enemy commander. This I proposed to remedy

"Hiya, remember me, shit head?"

I think it was the same one, Xiobargs all look alike to me.

"Yes, I remember you Earthman, very well. "

"You don't look so well. Is there anything I can do to help?"

"You can surrender now and I will not kill you, I will keep you as my personal slave.

"It depends, would I get time and a half for Saturdays and double time for Sundays or would you just use me as a sex toy, you beast?"

"I do not understand"

"In not surprised, what a dork you are. Has any of your race any intelligence at all or are they all as thick as you?"

He just stared at me. I got fed up looking at him.

"Remember what I said last time we met, well I've got a present for you, I've decided that I don't like you so I'm going to blow you away."

I turned round and ordered twenty rockets to be fired at his ship.

"Impossible; You could never get through my other ships. "

"Want to bet, their on their way. Ta Ta. "

Three of our rockets got through to his ship, one of the others hit a cruiser, the rest were destroyed. Pandemonium ran riot among the other enemy ships. Signals flew back and forth. A lot of them wanted to get away. They didn't like the idea of an enemy they couldn't see and

who could destroy them any time he chose. There were still over six hundred fighting ships left but frightened and leaderless they made easy targets. We had a field day. We let our rockets do most of the damage and as they tried to flee we sowed mines in their path. My freighters were let loose at last, much to their joy, on the Xiobarg transports. These we later found out were full of ground troops. We destroyed at least half of the original enemy fleet, the others managed to get away, unfortunately. we had been fighting for a week, everyone was shattered, We headed back to home world for a well earned rest. I waited for six months and, as there was no sign of the Xiobargs, I decided to carry out my plan for finding Earth"Another month and I was as ready as I would ever be.

that changed my mind about taking only one ship, I would take my mothership and two cruisers. I had Com search her memory banks with the intention of back tracking as far as she could. We wouldn't be in a rush so any new planets we found would be scanned and logged in Coms memory banks. We travelled without seeing any other life forms for months. One day we came upon what was left of the Blooran home world. It was a smoking ruin, completely devoid of life. The Xiobargs had made a really good job of it. My ships crews were gutted. We sailed on, we detoured now and then and sailed past planets and worlds that would, hopefully, one day be colonised by our people. Then one day we picked up a signal from a planet ahead. It was an Xiobarg ground base! They were reporting an attack on them by four Uxtomal ships! We had been flying without our cloaking device on, the place was full of enemies! We listened to them going on about how easy it had been to beat of the attack. I decided that the next attack they were involved in would be their last. I ordered the cruisers to attack. Keeping their cloaking devices on they swooped down and before the Xiobargs knew what was happening they were wiped out.

We picked up an incoming message directed at the base, They didn't get an answer, they kept trying though. I hoped they thought the Uxtomals were to blame. This was great! We could attack where we wanted and the Uxtomals and Xiobargs would blame each other. A week later we came upon five freighters escorted by two cruisers. As they were coming towards us I wondered if these were the originators of the signals we had picked up after destroying the base. We had our cloaking devices on so we just waited for them to come closer. The two cruisers went first. We jammed any signals the freighters might have made then I called them up. They had an assortment of materials and a few prisoners. There were only about twenty none Uxtomals in the prisoners so I had the Xiobargs put them aboard a shuttle and they flew to us. I had shut off the cloaking device on my ship but ordered the two cruisers to keep theirs on. When the prisoners were aboard my ship I ordered the Xiobärgs to leave. I also ordered my two cruisers to follow and destroy them. While waiting for the return of my cruisers we saw to the welfare of our new shipmates. As always they were in a pretty bad way. The Prof had insisted on coming along, for purely scientific reasons of course. For someone who was not violent, the Prof sure took delight in weapons that would cause devestating effects. He was telling me about an idea for a gas that would leave you retching your heart up till it finally killed you, He was hoping that when we got back from this expedition we could find a Xiobarg home world so he could try it out! We had travelled for weeks without sighting any enemy ships, we had picked up a lot of Xiobarg and Uxtonal signals. It seemed as if every enemy ship was being recalled from patrol duty. Something big was happening, but what, we had no idea. As we had been travelling we had dropped of some relay transmitters. We had placed them on moons and large asteroids. Being on desolate bodies, we hoped they would remain undetected. This enabled us to transmit, and receive messages from home world. For six months we made star charts and scanned new worlds. Com had always kept us roughly on our original course, back tracking. We approached one world and as we flex low across it certain features looked familiar to me. Suddenly, there on the screens, were the cliffs that Dundal and Septan had made their home! We completed our orbit and on our next one I ordered my ship to land. The nearest place was a plain about two miles from the cliffs. I and about a dozen of the ground troops set off towards the cliffs. I had one of the voice boxes with me. We had picked up life forms on our scanners and from the numbers it seemed that Dundal and Septan had been busy! My mind was full of these things and I had a smile on my face when I thought of Dundal and Septans reaction when they found out that I was the leader of this expedition. That was when, as we were walking through a defile full of brush and fallen rock, I was hit in the shoulder by an arrow! As I was falling I saw three of my men get hit. Two were hit by arrows ,the other by a stone. All three were dead! as two of my remaining men lifted me up, one was hit in the back by an arrow and I was shot in the leg. With the other men covering us we managed to pull back and with the help of a rescue team from the ship we managed to get back aboard without further loss. After I was patched up by the medics I asked if any of my men had seen who had attacked us. Nobody had seen anything, apart from the arrows and stones hitting us! I decided to stay on the planet and after my wounds had healed I would try again. It

took me seven weeks to recover. In that time anyone who ventured out side the ship was attacked. Our sensors were picking up life forms but we couldn't see anything! Stones and arrows seemed to come out of nowhere! On the day of my second attempt I had my men carry blast shields and wear helmets. I took twenty of the ground troops and as soon as we left the ship arrows and stones were bouncing of our shields. We had formed a defence screen which was similar to the old Roman testudo, the tortoise. It took us a good couple of hours to reach the cliffs. By this time everyones arms were just about dropping of with tiredness. We had suffered a few minor injuries as some of the stones had bounced under the shields and hit the men on the outside of the group on the legs and feet. I called a halt outside the caves that Dundal and Septan had made their home. There was no answer to my shouted calls. Instructing my men to form a defensive screen, I took five men with me and entered the cave. Everything was smashed or knocked over, the dust was inches thick. The cave hadn't been used for years! 1 searched around hoping to find some clue as to what had happened to them. Eventually, on a shelf about seven foot high I found a roll of parchment. When I unrolled it I found it was written in the form of a diary, this is what it said.

It is just over a week now since David left, Septan and I have been exploring. We have found a rock that when hit with a bear from an energy rifle burns for hours, there must be millions of tons of the rock so we have an unlimited fuel source.

2nd entry.

Today we explored the vast plain further, most of the plants and animals are ok to eat. We got back late but very happy with our new home. Most of the entry's were similar to this one until.

40th entry.

Xiobargs We nearly got caught! We had been so happy up till now. They surprised us, we were crossing the plain when their scout ship came out of nowhere and landed about half a mile from us. We dropped to the ground and luckily they didn't spot us. We had more luck, they turned away from the cliffs. They stayed for about five hours then left. They didn't seem to be doing anything. the soldiers just wandered about. We waited another hour before returning to our home in the cliffs. Our spirits are low, we will have to be more careful, our world has been spoiled.

50th entry.

Septan is pregnant! I'm going to be a father! She's due any day. She didn't tell me incase I wouldn't let her go exploring with me, silly girl.

52nd entry.f

It's twins! Two boys! Great! They are both tine and Septan is alright.

The next entries were about the boys growing up, Dundals people have a totally different growth rate to humans because within six months his children were running about and quite able to look after themselves, then disaster!

105th entry.

My boys! They have disappeared! They were playing outside the cave, I searched for hours till it got dark but there is no sign of them.

Septan is going crazy with worry. I will continue the search at first light Another thing is bothering me now that I think about it. For the last couple of days I have felt as though I was being watched, but I didn't see anything. Now I'm worried.

106th entry.

Dundal left to search for our boys over a week ago and he still hasn't returned. in going frantic with worry. First my beautiful boys and now Dundal. I can't wait any longer, I'm going to look for them. I will hide this journal incase I don't return either, If I don't find my boys and Dundal then I don't want to live.

With the state of the place, I guess none of them survived. My first two space friends, dead! I was saddened by the journal. I took a last look around then ordered a return too the ship. we hadn't gone very far when we were attacked again. I was thinking of Dundal and Septan when one of my men was hit by a ricocheting stone. At his cry of pain I became angry, I pulled the pin on a grenade and threw it into clump of bushes. The explosion tore the bushes apart, there was an ear shattering scream and something was flopping about on the ground. We advanced towards it. The arrows and stones had stopped but we didn't relax our vigilance one bit. As we got closer I could see our victim better. At first I thought it was a child but upon closer inspection It turned out to be a pigmy. As it was thrashing around it was rolling over shorn off branches, then the ground, then next to a large rock and each time it came in contact with the other it turned that colourI Chameleons As we watched it died. No wonder we couldn't see who was attacking us. Suddenly the arrows and atones started again. We reached our ship with only a few more bruises among us. I was a little saddened as we lifted off. Poor Dundal and Septan. If we had stayed together they might still be alive, There again if I had stayed with them on that planet I would probably be dead A sobering thought! We carried on with our expedition. We fell into our normal routine, one cruiser ahead on lookout duty. We didn't meet any enemy ships, but we came across planets that they had undoubtedly visited. Large cities destroyed, whole areas devastated and whole races killed. The Xiobargs and Uxtomas had a lot to answer for. After five month of wandering our lead ship reported a sizeable convoy of enemy ships ahead. Action at last. They turned out to be Uxtomals. We had our cloaking devises on and we joined the tail end of their fleet. It comprised of cruisers and two motherships. Twelve ships in total. On my command all three of my ships opened fire simultaneously. Three enemy cruisers blew up. We were, of course, monitoring their signals. Pandemonium! Their commander was screaming and shouting trying to regain command as everyone panicked! It was lovely to watch. Just as he was regaining some sort of order we blew up three more of his ships. Well that really set the cat amongst the pigeons. They all started firing at once. They were shooting all over the place, two of their own ships were damaged before the commander got them calmed down. We watched and waited.

"Who is firing on us, who are you? We are a peaceful race and wish you no harm. "

"Peaceful my arse" I had to answer him.

"You Uxtomals are a race of two faced liars and back stabbers and need wiping out! "

His face registered shock for we didn't show up on his scanners.

"You, you are a Terran! Your race dosen't have the capability of space flight, who are the others with you?"

Wouldn't you like to know. Well I haven't got time to talk to the likes of you all day so I'll say cheerio as it's time to kill you all." With that I ordered the attack. It didn't take long to finish them off. It was a little while later that I remembered the Uxtomal had known I was a Terran! SHIT! I could have got the Earths location from him! Double shit! That would have saved us a lot of time. Oh well, if there is one thing I've got lot of its time. we carried on with our search, The only thing I had told my crews about Earth was that it had a yellow sun and about nine other planets in the system. I had told them about Jupiter and it'e rings so hopefully that would be a good marker. Nobody saw anything or anyone for about three months when my lead cruiser reported a system ahead similar to the one we were looking for. With my heart racing I ordered full speed. We soon reached it and as my lead cruiser reported that there was only one planet capable of supporting our forms of life my hopes really soared. The cruiser was sending a more detailed report as we approached them. The surface had a lot of hot spot s mainly where cities had been located. My hopes and my heart dropped, it was obvious that the Uxtomals had been here. I posted a cruiser on lookout then had my ship orbit the Earth scanning for life forms. Most of the northern continents were radio active. The only thing I could put this down to was the Uxtomals destroying nuclear weapons and the resultant leak of radio active materials. We tried the southern hemisphere. The only place that wasn't hot was South America. We flew lower. There were signs of animal life but no humans. My hopes were as low as a snakes arse by this time and I sore revenge against all Uxtomals. I had just about given up when our sensors picked up human life forms on an island in the Mediterranean. It was one of the smaller islands just off Greece. I ordered an immediate landing. We chose the only level place we could find, about a mile from a small village. With my team I set off. This time we carried blast shields, I wasn't taking any chances. When we reached the village there was no sign of anyone, although fires were burning and food was cooking. I shouted that we were friends but understandably I got no reply. I could understand them being scared of the Uxtomals but I was a Terran, surly they could see the difference! It was as I was looking around that I took notice of my men. Of course! All my men were blue! I'd forgotten, I'd been with them that long I no longer noticed the difference. I ordered my men back to the ship but before we left I placed one of the translator boxes in the thatch of a hut. I left it there for two days then went back. The village was the same as before, signs of habitation but no people. I retrieved the box and returned to the ship. Com tried for four days to translate the language but didn't have any success. She asked me if I knew what it was but I didn't. It was all greek to me. Then it hit me! Greek of course, silly sod we were on one of the Greek islands! This knowledge still didn't help as I could not speak Greek. The only thing I could think of was to win their confidence, get them talking and hopefully learn some of the language for com to do a translation. I had one of my scout ships fly of to one of the larger continents and bring back a couple of wild cattle. These I would use as bait, I hoped that whilst they were cooking the smell would draw out the inhabitants of the village. When I'd got everything set up I ordered my men to return to the ship and wait. They were reluctant to leave me on by own but it was the only way that I could think of to gain the villagers confidence. I'd had other supplies brought to the village and I had a veritable feast going in no time. I kept in touch with my ship via radio. For four days nothing happened, I had caught occasional glimpses of someone but had had no clear sighting. On the fifth day I was rewarded by the sight of six villages approaching. They were very nervous but little by little they came nearer. I think it was the sight of so much food that gave them the courage to approach me. I had been wearing a blast shield on my back as a protection and always had a rifle close at hand. They were armed with spears and clubs. I motioned them to come closer and pointed at the food. Two of them were young men and it was these two who were the boldest. They came within twenty feet then stoped. I smiled at them and waved them closer They were whispering amongst themselves while the elder ones were clearly calling them back. I slowly stood up, with my hands empty. I thought they were going to run off. One

of then wanted to but the other just stood there watching me. Slowly I cut a piece of meat and offered it to him. He wasn't sure. I put the meat in a bowl and placed it on the ground then I stepped back a few paces and waited. Very slowly he advanced, his friend calling to him all the time. He came within six foot of the food and stopped, watching me. I moved slowly back. When I stopped he ran forward and grabbed the meat.

He turned and ran back to the village elders They stood there talking and the young lad was strutting about obviously saying how brave he had been. They looked back at me as I slowly walked up to the meat and cut off a piece. They watched me as I started to eat, They smelled the piece they had but again it was the youth who led the way. He took the meat back from the old man that had it and took a bite. They watched him, probably waiting for him to drop dead or something. They were amazed when he didn't. I squatted down in front of the fire I had lit and continued to eat. There was clearly an argument going on about what they should do. In the end the youth shouted something and began to walk towards me. As he came nearer and nearer I could see his resolve beginning to waver. I did everything slowly, I cut another piece oF meat and put it in the bowl. He came within ten feet then stopped. He was watching me very very carefully. I motioned for him to eat the meat then pretended to ignore him. As I didn't seem to be a threat he very slowly came forward. He picked up the meat and retreated about five yards. He squatted down and began to eat, he never took his eyes off of me all the time. Gradually he got closer and closer although I got the impression that I only had to say boo and he would have been up and running. As he was eating I studied him, He looked about eighteen and was my height, he wasn't as broad as me and he had the dark Greek colouring. His hair was long and matted. As we had been eating I had been smiling at him and now that we had finished I decided to try and talk to him. I told him my name and pointed at him. He jabbed his self in the chest and said "Nicos" I had a box with me and I set it on record. I then went through the motions of pointing at various things and having him tell me the Greek names. I kept at it for hours. He stayed all through the night and, as dawn was breaking, I contacted my ship to let them know that I was on my way back. As I stood up Nicos jumped back about ten foot! I smiled at him then turned and walked away. Once on the ship I got Com to make a language disc for the learning machine, then I did a session. The next day I returned to the village. Nicos was waiting for me. As I approached he held up his hand in greeting. The look on his face when I spoke to him in is own language was a sight to see. Total amazement! I explained that I was an Earth man like him and that I had been kidnapped by the Uxtomals. I then asked him what had happened to the Earth and all it's people. He wasn't sure but said that the village elders knew as the story had been handed down from father to son for generations.

Generations! God, have I been away that long. He said he would fetch the others and he disappeared into the country side. He was gone for hours When he returned, he had the same people with him as before. Nicos came straight up to me and sat down , the others were more cautious. They eventually came near, with me talking, encouraging them in their own language, Nicos, on the other hand, was calling them all sorts of names.

All the food from the previous days had disappeared. I asked the elder if it was alright for my men to bring more. At first they wanted to leave but Nicos brow beat them into staying. As my men were stacking the food, I could tell the villages thought we would fall on them and make them prisoners. Even Nicos was nervous but he had to put a brave face on. Once my men left, everyone relaxed. The food was served out and as we ate I asked the elders what had happened. They told me that the legends were the Uxtomals had contacted the big governments of the world with offers of peace and cooperation. Then they had started to sow the seed of discontent. The result of this was a world war. Nuclear weapons had been used, killing most of the northern hemispheres population. The Uxtomals had then taken the survivors prisoner and had attacked and subdued the southern hemisphere, The small number who had escaped all this then had to put up with climatic changes in order to survive The Uxtomals had returned on odd occasions to look for survivors. One thing had been passed down , Watch for danger from the skies. We talked on into the night and I could see Nicos and a couple of the younger ones were fascinated by my stories of space and what I had seen. As the day had progressed, more and more of the villagers had come out of hiding. There were about forty of them ranging from the very young to the very old. There were seven about Nicos's age, three of whom were girls. It was just before dawn that I received a message of the appearance of two Uxtomal cruisers. When I passed on this info to the villagers they jumped up and began to run. Nicos was unsure what to do. I was still sat by the fire and was unconcerned. He hesitated then asked what I was going to do. I answered his question with a question.

"What are you going to do? Are you going to hide for the rest of your life or are you going to fight?"

He looked at me then looked where the others had run. I could see the indecision in his face. He took a deep breath then sat down.

"Good lad. Will any of the others fight if I give you the weapons?"

"I'm not sure but I will ask them. Now, will you fight them?"

"Just leave that to me, you go and bring back as many as you can and I will meet you here in half a days time. Don't worry about the Uxtomals." I returned to my ship and after giving the captain instructions I collected six blast rifles and some other equipment and returned to the village. I hadn't long to wait. Nicos returned with one of the young men and the three girls. I was a little bit disappointed but it was a start. Nicos told me that although the others wouldn't come out of hiding they would watch to see what happened. Well that was better than nothing. I gave a rifle to each of them and showed them how to use them. All we had to do now was wait. I had given instructions to my crew to take at least a dozen prisoners and to destroy the rest along with their ships. I told Nicos and the others to look up into the sky and watch. We hadn't long to wait before there was a bright flare then about an hour later another. My radio crackled into life, reporting that both enemy ships were destroyed and, about the capture of eighteen Uxtomal prisoners. I ordered the captain to bring the prisoners to my location. Nicos and the others were staring at the radio as if it would bite them, so I explained what it was. They seemed a lot happier after. They got nervous when the Uxtomals wore brought into the village. I think if it hadn't been for Nicos the others would have run away. The look of awe on their faces when I spoke to the Uxtomals was something else. I told Nocos and his friends that the Uxtomals had been charged with crimes against all peoples and races and that the penalty for their crimes was death. Nicos and the others just looked at me. I stepped forward and grabbed the nearest Uxtomal and lifted him of the ground. I threw him about thirty feet away. When Nicos and the others saw this they looked at me with fear on their faces. I told Nicos to do the same. He looked at me then at the others, fear and indecision on his face. I started to deride him.

"What's the matter Nicos! Frightened?Are you a man or what?Its easy to talk big in front of your friends, eh?Are you going to hide all your life, are you going to let someone else do all your fighting for you? I thought you had more guts." I turned my back on him and spoke to one of the Blooran females that was waiting with the guards, She came forward and handed her weapons to me. Then she turned and grabbed an Uxtomal. She threw him onto the ground and with practiced ease broke his neck. I looked back at Nicos. All his life he had been told about the aliens and had grown up fearing them, now he had just seen one killed by a woman! Hesitantly he walked forward and hit the nearest Uxtomal. The result really surprised him, he had expected the Uxtomal to stagger or fall, like I had all those years ago. When the Uxtomal sailed through the air and landed about ten to twelve feet away, he was amazed. I tried to explain about gravity and the differences on our world and the enemy world. I don't think he was listening, he kept staring at his fist. The others were chattering amongst themselves when Nicos hit another Uxtomal. This one went even further, Nicos was really please with himself. The Uxtomals were cowering, begging for their lives. No chance. I turned to Nicos and told him to kill them. The smile left his face but the determination was there. He raised his rifle and shot the first one he'd hit. He then turned to his companions and told them to do the same. The rest of the villagers had come a little closer whilst all this was going on and as the Uxtomass began to panic, then run, their fear turned to hatred and the chase was on. They killed the Uxtomals with their spears, stones and even their bare hands. We had a great feast that night to celebrate, The next day I had more rifles brought to the village and we showed the villages how to use them. When it was time to go I asked if anyone wanted to come with us. Nicos was the first to say yes, I knew he would, but I was a bit disappointed when the three girls were the only others to volunteer. Ah well. It was a start. We returned to the ship. Nicos was strutting around but the girls were still nervous. I got Nicos to take the language discs first and the look on his face when he realised that he could understand everything that was being said was a picture to see, He then helped me to reassure the girls that it was quite painless. They had the same look on their faces afterwards. I then showed them around the ship. It was like introducing a couple of kids to a toy store. They seemed a little frightened by it all but were reassured when I told them that the disc would put it all into perspective. They soon began to relax, that is, till I showed them the Earth through a view port. They couldn't believe that tiny speck was the Earth. I showed them to their quarters and where the galley was then left them to get settled in. I returned to the bridge. The prof asked me if I was happy now that I had found my home world. I was upset at what had happened to the Earth and there was no consolation in the knowledge that the same had happened to other worlds. The only thing was that my resolve had depend about the Uxtomals and the Xiobargs. No race would be safe until they were wiped out completely. We set our course for home world. During the trip back Nicos and the three girls, Anna, Karina ad Liona were frequent visitors to the disc machine, They were acquiring vast amounts of knowledge very quickly. Within four months they were wanting to do a proper job of work. Nicos wanted to join the ground troops and the girls wanted to learn the bridge stations. They were very eager. I turned them over to the relevant section commanders for training. After a few months I met Nicos by accident in one of the hangers. I walked up to him to ask how he was doing. He came to attention and saluted me. I was a little taken aback at this and before I could say anything his commanding officer said that private Nico was doing well. I mumbled something or other, saluted then left. I was a little saddened to think Nicos was now just another subordinate. In all fairness I couldn't treat him any different to any other crewman. I then thought of the girls. Damn it! I had been having a few dreams lately about restarting the human race I would have to think of something and fast. I know, I will invite one of the girls to dinner. Yes thats it, but which one! I was still pondering this as I entered the bridge and it was a while before I noticed the stares I was getting. None essential personnel had come to attention .They were waiting for me to return their salute and say, carry on. some of them were used to my quaint erratic ways and just smiled in a knowing way, I walked over to where the girls were receiving instruction from the sensor operator. As I walked over they came to attention and saluted. They stood there looking straight forward. I stilll didn't know which one to invite so I invited all of them on the pretext that I wanted to discuss something with them, Then I was striving to find a subject I could talk to them about ! Damn! On the flight back to home world we found two abandoned Uxtomal bases. There seemed to be no reason for them to have left. This was very curious. While I was trying to figure this out I completely forgot my dinner arraignment. When the girls turned up at my quarters I was a little surprised till Anna said I had invited them. I got them drinks and sat them down, then because I couldn't think of any thing else to say I asked them to tell me about themselves. Anna went first. Her parents had been taken by the Uxtomals so one of the other villagers had brought her up and she was hoping that Nicos was going to marry her! One down. Karina went next. She and Liona were sisters and the best news of all, Nicos was there brother! We talked in general for the rest of the night, the only thing I remember was I kept thinking that two out of three wasn't bad! The days went by and I saw more and more of Karina and Liona. The relationship seemed to be going well. We had been picking up Uxtomal signals for some time, they were all the same. General recall of all ships! What was going on? Must be something big. A few months later we reached home world. What a difference! We now had cities where there had been towns, more factories and the space port was ten times bigger! When I had landed Charlie

, Lank, Barney and Starn all came to see me and welcome me home. I congratulated them on there endeavours. Charlie and Barney were parents! They wanted me to be a godparent, I could only accept. They asked about my trip and I told them over dinner. The local news was good, they hadn't been any contact with the Xiobargs and forty new ships had been built in our own factories. The population had soared with the original people being given the longevity drug their children were passed on some of the benefits, they were living longer and so were their children. One of the first things I had done was to give my earth friends the drug. There was only five of us so we had to survive. There might be some earth survivors among the Uxtomal prisoners but I couldn't take the chance of finding any. The vast majority of our populace were Bloorans with Numals being the next largest. There was the odd Cammeel and one or two other aliens that I didn't know the name of, Earthmen were least numerous. Thoughts like these were going through my mind and yet I was the leader! Amazing! Its a funny old world. For a year since my return, things had been quiet. when I say quiet, I mean there had been no sign of the Xiobargs. This wasn't a bad thing, it's just that I had this feeling that it wouldn't last. In that time I had got married. I couldn't make up my mind who to ask, Karina or Liona. In the end I did the only thing I could do. I married them both! Well we all have to make sacrifices for the good of the race. For the last six months I had been in constant demand from both my wives. This is what happens when your fantastic in bed. I don't think it was charisma, I was the only human male around! Karina wanted an immediate family while Liona wanted to further her career in the fleet. Nicos had married, he and Anna had a baby on the way. A further year went by and I was getting bored! There wasn't anything I could do really, apart from domestic duties! I decided the time had come for an expedition. The thought that kept crossing my mind was the Xiobargs were up to something , but what. I decided it was time to find out. We now had thirty brand new ships so I gave orders that twelve of them should be fully provisioned as soon as possible. These ships were all motherships and had all the latest weaponry and sensors. We would be a match for anything the Xiobargs had, It took a further six months to get everything ready. I said goodbye to Karinna, she was staying behind as she was pregnant. Liona was to be a crew member on my ship. Rank hath its privileges Charlie, being a mother, had to stay behind and Starn was civilian in charge. Barney and Lank both wanted to come along. I tossed a coin, figuratively speaking, and Barney won. Lank would be in charge of home fleet. Barney would be second in command on the expedition. We decided to try our luck in a sector we had not been in before. We had of course charted the stars and planets around us for five weeks cruising in all directions. We felt fairly safe up to this distance. After that, who knew. We kept our cloaking devices on at all times. We charted and explored for six months with only the discovery of four abandoned Xiobarg bases to relieve the boredom. We couldn't find any reason why these bases had been abandoned. We sailed on. As on my trip to find the Earth, we left beacons on various asteroids and moons.

When I began to think the Xiobargs had all disappeared and we were wasting our time, our lead ship picked up a transmission. It was from a Xiobarg fleet informing a ground base that they were bringing them supplies and reinforcements. Action at last! All ships were put on alert and we homed in on the Xiobargs, As we got closer we could see that the enemy fleet comprised of four motherships and a dozen cruisers. There were thirty freighters with them. This would be easy. As we came in range we began jamming their signals.We also scanned the freighters for signs of prisoners. The only life forma we detected besides the Xiobargs were Uxtomals, thousands of them! Telling my captains to leave the enemy flag ship alone, we attacked. The freighters took no time at all to destroy and the Xiobarg cruisers didn't last much longer. I called a cease fire when the enemy commander had only one ship besides his own left. I had a communication link opened to his ship.

"Hello, are you having trouble old chap?"

"You! I should have known when my ships began to blow up. "

"Oh you know me do you, I would have remembered if I'd ever met you before as you have such a distinguished countenance. "

"All my people know of you Terran. You and all your people would have been eliminated long ago if we had not been distracted by the Uxtomals"

"So that's what you have been up to is it. Well I hope they caused you some serious damage and you them. "

I wanted to keep him talking, I had to find out what had happened.

"They resisted for some time but we have defeated them now. They didn't fight like we did. They were frightened and uncommitted. Now we rule their world and bases. The ones we didn't kill have become our slaves." He seemed pleased with himself.

This was good news indeed! One less enemy to deal with. He continued.

"Now we can concentrate on you. You will not last long. we do not tolerate interference in our conquest of space. You and the Bloorans cannot stop us. We have new weapons that will destroy you all. These weapons have been tested on Terran and Blooran prisoners and are very effective indeed. "

The Xiobargs must have got the Terran prisoners from the captured Uxtomal bases! The Xiobargs overran the Blooran world themselves.

"I hope the Uxtómals caused you a lot of casualties in ships and troops"

"When they saw the size of our invasion fleet a lot of them surrendered without a fight. We captured a lot of their ships intact and some were only slightly damaged, It didn't take us long to repair them. We have, of course, pressed them into our service. We have had to use the Uxtomal crews but the officers are Xiobarg. We are invincible. "

I let him ramble on, my mind was trying to absorb all this information New weapons, a vast increase in their fleet. Jesus! this wasn't good at all.

I ordered the information to be sent back to home world with a warning to be doubly alert. I dragged my mind back and tried to concentrate on what the enemy commander was saying. He was still bragging about how good the Xiobargs were. I'd heard it all before. He told mo to surrender and he would see to it that after being paraded around his world I would be executed quickly. I asked about the treatment my crews could expect. They would be put to work for the greater glory of the Xiobargs He waited while I thought about his offer, he thought I was going to accept! The look on his face when I said "Destroy them." was comical. I contacted Barney and discussed this news with him. I decided that we would press on and try to learn more. We went deeper into enemy space.

While we searched I thought of what the Xiobarg commander had said. It was obvious that the Xiobargs were now in possession of all the Uxtomal information and locations of all the worlds and planets that the Uxtomals had ever visited. This meant that the Earth would also be known to them. Because of me they would destroy it. This really got me down. There was nothing I could do. The future looked very bleak indeed.

After about a month we detected a large defence screen ahead. I sent a ship to investigate. The rest of us waited. The captains report was short and to the point. He had scouted the defence screen and had detected the movement of a large body of ships. He had tagged along behind them, through the screen, and was in orbit near a large planet that his sensors indicated was an Xiobarg home world! I told him to hold his position and guide us in, we were on the way. With our cloaking devices on we passed through the screen without incident. we closed up with our scout ship and watched the Xiobargs. There were a lot of ships of all sizes landing and taking off. If we succeeded in destroying this planet, the Xiobargs might just leave us alone. That is what I hoped as I ordered the attack. Most of my ships would engage the shipping while four would attack the cities. It was a rush plan and I was counting heavily on the element of surprise. With ships coming and going we would not be able to block all the signals. We could cause a lot of confusion with the blocking of most of them. Barney led the attack on the cities while I led the attack on the shipping. My shout of tallyho and up and at em caused some puzzled looks, even from Liona. I didn't have time to explain as we engaged the first ship in our path. They didn't know what hit them. There were a number of space ports so I had split my ships into four groups of two. As we shot down the enemy ships we listened to their signals. Some of the ships had Uxtomal crews and these were being blamed for the attack. With us blocking their signals they couldn't verify or deny this. Pandemonium! Enemy ships were firing all over the place. Any ship that came in range of another fired first. when their cities came under attack they realised that it was an outside force doing the attacking, but, as they couldn't see us they didn't know what to do. It was inevitable that some ships would escape. We could still monitor their signals but they were out of range of our blocking them. They started to call for help. I instructed my ships to do as much damage as they could for another half an hour then to break off. We would rendezvous at our starting point. We were just pulling out when we picked up a very large explosion from the vicinity of the biggest Xiobarg city. When we all gathered I counted heads. One ship was missing. It was Barney's ship! No one had seen what had happened. He was swooping in for a final attack when the explosion had occurred. After that there was no sign of his ship We repeatedly called him, but there was no answer. Barney! One of my longest friends, dead! I ordered the withdrawal back to our home world with a heavy heart. What would I tell his wife. My crew were jubilant. Countless enemy ships and cities destroyed. It was a great victory. I couldn't join in the celebrations just yet though. We passed through the defence screen and as we did so I ordered it destroyed. I wanted the Xiobargs to feel vulnerable for a change. We had been on our way home for a week when our sensors detected a ship following us. We had our cloaking device on so I decided to wait and see who it was. Imagine my surprise and delight when it turned out to be Barneys ship. He hadn't seen us and would have passed right by us if we hadn't called him. His ship had sustained a lot of damage. This had been caused by the explosion. I had him ferried across to by ship and had him tell me the whole thing. When his ship had attacked the city on his final run he had noticed a large building as yet untouched. He had fired at it in passing. It must have contained a large amount of explosives. His ship was blown arse over tit into space by the force of the blast. When they had stopped spinning and brought some semblance of order to the chaos the rest of us where nowhere in sight. He then found out most of his sensors and communicators were not working. Luckily his clocking device was. A lot of his crew were

injured, some seriously, so he had decided to head for home and here he was! He had a broken arm and several cracked ribs. I arranged for some of the crewmen off of the other ships to replace Barneys people and we continued home. Now I joined in the celebrations! We had scored a great victory and with most if not all of an Xiobarg home world destroyed the enemy might just leave us alone. We reached our home world in due course without any mishaps. When we told our people the good news the celebrations lasted a full week! Time passed without any sign of the Xiobargs and we were happily working away. Some of the rescued aliens wanted to start their own colonies so it was decided that we would set them up on their own planets. We had, during our forays, found four planets that were habitable within a week to a month cruising time. These we decided would become home worlds 2, 3, 4, 5. Home world 2 would be for the less numerical races such as Terrans, Cammeels and the Mordons. The Mordons resembled the Bloorans more than any other race, They were a lighter blue and their features were regular. The main differences were they had claws instead of fingers and they didn't breathe through their mouths, they extracted oxygen through their skins There were about forty of them. Home world 3 would be for the Numal and 4 and 5 would be for the over flow of Bloorans who made up 80% of our population. Our ship production was coming along fine, and as the new worlds were in a half moon shape around home world, it was decided that the bulk of the fleet would remain here. There hadn't been any sightings of enemy activity so it was decided to step up production of the freighters. Being smaller than a fighting ship we could produce three a week! The freighters were, of course armed. No point in taking chances, they could fight if needed. For months freighters flew back and forth between world 1 and the other worlds carrying first people then materials. The first thing to be set up was a defence grid, then living quarters. For the first year everything came from home world 1. After that the new worlds started to become self sufficient. We were thriving! Our population expanded at an alarming rate, especially the Bloorans. The Numals were next. I of course tried to out do them all! Everyone was happy. We had colonised three more planets, mainly for the Bloorans and our little federation was prospering. In five years we had 8 major worlds and a couple of smaller bases. We also had a couple of moons that we used as ammunition dumps. The Prof and his rapidly expanding team of scientists were developing weapons at an alarming rate. Some of the people wanted to stop weapons production and turn the industries to more peaceful things. As I was still the leader or, as some put it. the President, I refused this request. I also made sure that at least one out of five ships built was a fighting ship. The Xiobargs, I had to admit, were quiet but I didn't believe for one minute that they had forgotten about us. Each race had made a contribution to our way of life, from the artistic to the functional. Freighters plied back and forth with all sorts of goods aboard. I also made sure that each and everyone had at least one years service in our armed forces, Our democracy grew. Each world chose three representatives for the council which met four times a year. There was one Terran, me, one Cammeel, a Mordon, three Numals and eighteen Bloorans. So far I had always got my way regards arms and fighting ships but some of the reps were young and had only heard about the Xiobargs. They were the ones that believed we were safe. They had me scared, Three more years went by without a sign that the Xiobargs had ever existed. Through the years we had created holidays, one such day was a celebration of our victory over the Xiobarg home world. The celebrations were in full swing when I received a call from fleet headquarters. We still maintained a ship on lookout duty, although I had to fight to keep it there. They had spotted an unmarked and unmanned

probe headed towards home world They had blocked any signals it was sending and wanted to know if they should destroy it or capture it. I sent them a message advising extreme caution, On no account was it to be brought aboard their ship, till it had been extensively examined. We waited anxiously for their reply. They sent a shuttle across to it as their tractor beam held it. Before they could even get close the thing exploded. Luckily no one was injured. When we received this message I had a premonition of impending danger. I ordered a full alert of all our forces and the assembly of our full fleet at home world 1. A meeting of the council was called and I told them of my fears. Some of the younger ones were sceptical, They believed that with over 5000 fighting ships and our weapons we could easily defeat any size fleet the Xiobargs might send against us. As president of the council I told them that I was ordering all industries to go to weapon production immediately. They complained bitterly, saying that I was over reacting to the appearance of one unidentified probe. I brushed aside all their arguments and also informed them that they had better report for active service. I had all the freighters report to the arms dumps and load up. A quarter of them were filled with nothing else but mines, the rest with everything else.

For a week nothing happened, we sowed our mines and waited. The first indication that the Xiobargs were really after us was when we picked up one of their signals. Their commander informed all his captains that no prisoners were to be taken except the leaders if possible. He told them all that a reward was being offered for the Terran, dead or alive. It's nice to know your wanted. As they got closer we could see the full extent of their fleet. I was proud of the size of my fleet but the Xiobarg fleet made ours look like a scouting party by comparison! I had 4500 ships at my command, most of which were motherships. I had left the others as a guard around our home worlds. The Xiobargs got closer and closer and the full extent of their fleet became apparant. Wave after wave, thousands and thousands of ships. Over 50000 and not one of them a freighter! Deep shit! Our freighters had just sown the third lot of mines when the lead enemy ships ran into our mine field. The whole Xiobarg fleet came to a stop. We were monitoring their signals. Their commander ordered the ships with Uxtomal crews to advance. His intention was clear. He was going to us them to clear a path through the mines. Although they couldn't detect our mines with their sensors they had come up against them before. They had also used the years between our last meeting to advantage. They used some sort of ray to explode the mines, sweeping back and forth to create a path through which their ships could advance. This they had to do at a snails pace. We fired our rockets at them. Most were destroyed but yet again the Xiobargs had a answer.Their tracking system must have been improved, they fired at the precise location of the ship that fired the rockets! We lost a cruiser. They must have back tracked the rocket. This was getting worse by the minute. The enemy were nearly through the mine field, I ordered my ships to attack. We had to contain them in the narrow corridor between the mines or we might as well give up. Once they spread out we would be over whelmed, Even with our cloaking devices we were hard put to contain them. The first enemy ships were easy to destroy as they were the ones with Uxtomal crews. They didn't have the stomach to fight. When we got to the Xiobargs things were different. They were awesome fighters, they knew no fear at all. We fought all day and night, if your ship wasn't destroyed after twelve hours of continuous fighting you would be pulled back for a rest and to tend to the injured, Then it was back into the fight again. After three days the Xiobarg commander realised that he wasn't going to break through at that point. He ordered his ships to make holes in our mine field at four other places. The gap that we were currently defending had got bigger and bigger due mainly to disabled ships blundering into other mines. It was not big enough for fifty ships to pass through. Motherships that is. The Xiobargs had also improved their defence screens, they wern't as easy to knock out as they used to be. All my ships had been in the fighting and the crews were getting tired, the enemy had not used even half of his force yet! We watched anxiously as more gaps were being punched in our mine field. All I could do was get the freighters to sow more and more mines at the points the Xiobargs looked like breaking through at.The reports from home world was that the ammunition factories were at peak production. I now had half of our freighters sowing mines, I also had the freighter crews swop with some of our fighting crews. I split my ships into three divisions, I commanded one and Barney and Lank the others. This was supposed to give us at least a full days rest. After a weeks solid fighting the original gap was now wide enough for a hundred ships abreast! The other gaps were getting wider and deeper but as yet the enemy hadn't broken through. It was only a matter of time. We had just repulsed another attack when we picked up a message from the Xiobarg commander, it was directed at me.

"I wish to talk to the Terran, I know that you are in charge of the ships opposing us. You cannot win this battle, we are too strong. "

I didn't reply to his taunts. I was too busy listening to the reports that were flooding in. Reports of casualties and ship losses, fatigue and shortages getting worse by the minute. Our freighters were still sowing the mines and bringing much needed supplies but their crews were also suffering. Our home worlds were at maximum output now and couldn't keep up with demand. We had recieved three new motherships since we had joined battle with the Xiobargs, but we had lost over two hundred destroyed or too severely damaged to carry on fighting. I had

asked the Prof if he and his team could come up with anything but as yet they hadn't. We needed time, desperately I was issuing orders and trying to think of some way to gain the time we needed when the enemy commander repeated his message. I decided to hear what he wanted to say.

Even a few minutes rest would be welcome. I ordered a channel opened.

"Ok dogs breath, what is it you want. Make it quick, We've got Xiobargs to kill. "

"You cannot defeat us, we are too strong. "

"Is that it! You've already said that. You are just wasting my time, aren't you. I thought you had something important to say."

He seemed a little put out by this. He probably expected me to be quaking in my boots, instead he had got the opposite reaction to the one he wanted. Just to upset him further I ordered meat for dinner and told the duty officer that I would have it cooked to the same colour as the Xiobarg commanders face. While I was winding up the Xiobarg, Barneys ships took over from us in the front line. The enemy commander looked as if he was ready to explode. I decided to cut him off.

"Well I can't stand here all day looking at your ugly mug, Iv'e got a party to go too tonight and Iv'e got to wash my hair. See you around. "

I got a reaction but not one that I wanted. He split his force and sent about ten thousand ships to find a way around our mine field, This meant that I had to split my forces as well. I sent Lank and his ships to shadow them. I also gave him a third of the mine laying freighters. We were spread mighty thin now and the out come was inevitable. We might be able to hold them for another week but I wasn't confident we could.

It looked like the end of our federation. We could only fight on! we were destroying or disabling two to three of the enemy ships for everyone of ours lost. There was so many of the enemy ships that only a half had actually been in the battle while we were more or less constantly in the fighting. The prof had come up with a new weapon, it was a cannon that fired glass capsules of acid. we knocked out a couple of enemy ships with them but the stuff was a danger to our ships as well. It could be used to block holes in the mine field, I thought, but when we tried it it just dissolved the mines around the cloud. If a shot exploded in or near a cloud of acid it scattered it all over the place. The stuff was more of a liability than an asset. We were still being pushed back, the enemy line was getting longer and longer. I couldn't see any way we were going to stop the Xiobargs. The only thing left to do was evacuate our home worlds and run. Lank had only succeeded in delaying the Xiobargs on his front for a day then they broke through his lines. He was trying to stop them and asked if I could send him any reinforcements. I had to tell him no. Barney and myself were fighting a loosing battle as well.

I ordered all freighters to sow their mines and to return to home world were they were to start loading civilians ready to evacuate. I informed all ships captains that they were to hold up the Xiobargs as long as was possible. Our home worlds had, of course, been monitoring our signals and the battle and no one was under any delusions as to what would happen when the Xiobargs got to our planets. The evacuation went smoothly but it still took over two days to get everyone and everything that would be needed on board the freighters and away. My entire fleet was scattered. My crews were in a daze, all our hopes gone! Lank was trying his best to slow down his enemy fleet and stop my ships from being cut off and surrounded. I ordered a faster retreat. As soon as the Xiobargs realised that we were pulling out they increased their speed. We still needed to give our freighters a good lead so every now and then we would turn and fight. The enemy poured more and more ships through the gap in our mine field, I had lost over half of my ships by this time, the Xiobargs had lost four times as many but still had over 30,000 ships in their fleet. When the last freighter had lifted of our home planets the defences were put on automatic. I was hoping that this would give us a little time to break away,.We kept retreating, turning now and then to fight. The effect this had on the Xiobargs was to make them fight harder. It was like trying to stop a charging bull with a fly swatter! Three more days of this kind of fighting and we could see home world 1 on our long range scanners. Lanks ships had rejoined us but our front line was way too thin. There were now twenty odd thousand enemy ships against two thousand of ours.

As we got closer to our home world the Xiobarg commander called me up.

"So Terran, I have you now. Nowhere else to run. I am going to enjoy destroying your home, and family. You have been a great annoyance to us but now it is over. You and those Bloorans will cease to exist. "

I laughed. He didn't know what to make of this, neither did my crew.

"Do you seriously think you've beaten us! This was just a warm up for the real thing. You just wait till we really get going. What do you think will happen when we have a fleet as big as yours. What will your superiors say when they find out that a fleet that was less than a tenth of your size out fought you for a week or more and that you failed to destroy it. I wouldn't be so cocky if I were you. The mighty and all powerful Xiobargs indeed! Ha. You are so scared of us that you darn't fight us one to one on equal terms. The next time we meet it will be different. "

I cut off the link with him before he could say anything. I wanted him to be so mad that he would want to annihilate our home planets rather than keep coming after us. We continued with our hit and run tactics.

When I received word from the freighters that they were safely out of danger I ordered all ships to disengage from the enemy and run like hell It was depressing to watch on our screens the destruction of our homes but at least we were alive. We took every precaution to leave no trail that the Xiobargs could follow. Our freighters were sending a signal to us on a tight beam and we zeroed in on this. We caught them up five days later. Our ships were being run by skeleton crews while we tried to recuperate. We knew the Xiobargs would try to catch us but for the moment we didn't care. I had left one ship behind as a rear lookout. His orders were to watch and monitor the Xiobargs. I wanted as much notice of the Xiobargs coming after us as I could get. The first thing our scout reported was the finding and destroying of everyone of our home worlds. The Xiobargs lost some ships to our ground defence networks but once they realised they were unmanned they stood back and poured long range fire on them till they were obliterated. Our scout ship was also instructed to detonate the ammunition dumps when any Xiobarg ships were close enough, the more the merrier. Once our worlds had been destroyed, the Xiobaergs spread out to try and find our trail. Our scout ship stayed at extreme sensor range and watched. Five days later, we lost our scout. The Xiobargs had detected something, and were starting to group up on to our trail. Our scout decided to swing around the enemy fleet and to engage their opposite flank. When he was in position he opened fire with all weapons. He had destroyed three ships and disabled one other while drawing them away when he was detected and then destroyed. Having got our scouts last message that he was under attack and then silence, we got under way. I left another ship behind as a look out with orders to watch for five days and if there wasn't any sign of the Xiobargs they were to catch us up as quickly as possible. I was toying with the idea of swinging back in a circle to get behind the Xiobargs. My reasoning being that they would keep looking for us no matter how long it took. If we doubled back we might just avoid them long enough to recuperate The best place to rest up would be where the Xiobargs had already been. Even it we did encounter any enemy ships I felt confident that they would only be a handful of them. With the freighters I still had a force of six thousand ships, the freighters were a match for any Xiobarg cruiser. I discussed this with Barney and Lank. They agreed with my reasoning. We set off in a vide arc, hopefully this would take us beyond any Xiobarg scouts. I had scouts out on both flanks and in front, the scout we had left to guard our backs was informed and given our next heading. I was trying to find a planet that the Xiobargs had been to but hadn't stayed at. Our people were getting anxious at being cooped up on the freighters for so long but they knew there wasn't anything else to do. Food wasn't a problem yet, neither was water but it wouldn't be too long before they were. Within a week we had found a planet that would support our life forms. It was one that the Xiobargs had had a ground base on and we had destroyed it. They hadn't rebuilt it so hopefully they

wouldn't be back. After leaving scouts well out in space, to give us time to reembark our people if the enemy were sighted heading this way, we landed on the planet surface. Camps were soon set up and a happy spirit seemed to invade us all. We had only been on the planet a week and some of the younger people were talking about setting up a permanent base! I couldn't believe it. Just because the Xiobargs hadn't found us yet they thought we were safe. In the middle of enemy territory! Good God! If I didn't put a stop to this kind of thinking they'd be wanting to talk to the Xiobarge about living in peace. Didn't they understand anything that had happened to us at all! The only peace we could expect from the Xiobargs was the kind you got from being dead! While I was arguing with them about this I had a piece of luck, if you can call it luck. The Xiobargs found us, well, we found them actually. They didn't know we were there. one of our scouts reported an enemy fleet of five hundred ships approaching.

As they were still two days away we had plenty of time to load up our freighters and lift off from the planets surface. Once our freighters were at a safe distance I ordered my fighting ships to surround the enemy fleet. We stayed at extreme sensor range. we monitored their signals and waited to see what they would do. I didn't want to tip our hand if it wasn't necessary. They didn't seem to be in any hurry to get where they were going, we just tagged along. After a day and a half it was obvious.

They were heading straight for the planet we had been on. As soon as they saw it they would know we had been there and would send for the main fleet straight away. We had to have time at all costs. I ordered the attack. The Xiobargs had been busy, They had improved their sensors, they picked us up as soon as they picked up our signs on the planets surface. From their signals they knew who we were straight away. We began blocking their distress call to their main fleet. This proved harder than before, they obviously had improved this as well! We had to destroy them as quickly as possible. The longer we took to do this the less time we would have of evading any following force. With this in mind we gave them everything we had. Rockets from long range, then lasers when we got close. Even though we out numbered them two to one it wasn't one sided. We took a few oF their ships out with the rockets but they had improved their defences so much that a long range battle would have taken us weeks to win. We had to get close. Although they could see us with their sensors they couldn't see us on their view screens. This didn't really matter because this type of battle was fought by the computers. The computers were fed information by the life form concerned such as which type of weapon to use and which type of ammunition, the life form was a spectator really, The Xiobargs used their star shells to good effect, every now and then one of our ships would appear on the view screen, although the image was distorted you could see it. It took us a full day of hard fighting to defeat the enemy fleet. At the end of the battle we had lost another three hundred and forty ships. We hadn't even managed to stop

147

all their distress calls either. After making sure our own disabled ships were clear of wounded we destroyed them. I didn't want the Xiobarga to get any information from their computers. With heavy hearts we set out after our freighters. We had to get as far away as possible, this part of space would be crawling with enemy ships before too long. We were back to square one, running! Everyone was depressed. With the longevity drug, I'd got forever to run, unless I was killed by the Xiobargs. A really bright future! We soon caught up to the freighters and with scouts out all around our fleet we sailed onwards. We avoided all planets that had signs of Xiobarg occupancy, no point in advertising our whereabouts. I think we all knew that the Xiobargs would find us eventually and that it would be the end. Some of us might escape but a life of running didn't appeal to anyone. Food was our main concern, we could recycle our water more or les indefinitely but only manufacture certain types of food. To this end we were constantly on the look out for uninhabited worlds. We had just left such a world after sailing for two months when our forward scout sent us a report of a large unidentified ship which seemed to be helpless. As we approached this ship Com identified it as a Cammeel mothership! What was it doing here? I thought they'ed all dime warped years back I got our scout to scan for life forms and when he had I was amazed to find it was full of Cammeels. I contacted Lank and told him to speak to them if he could before we switched off our cloaking devices. Lank spoke to them for hours. At first they didn't believe that it could be him. They thought he was dead, they had seen his ship knocked out in their battle with the Xiobargs all those years ago. After assuring them that he wasn't dead he told them what had happened since. We invited their commander on to my ship. Their ship had had engine trouble and was unable to dime warp.

They had been anxiously scanning space for signs of any enemy when Lank had suddenly spoken to them. Not being able to see us they had nearly died of fright While we had been talking to the Cammeel commander our engineers had been on his ship to help repair his engines. As he was about to leave, I had a sudden thought which filled me with hope. I asked the Cammeel commander if we could copy his dime warp device. If we could do this we could escape from the Xiobargs! During our talk he had told us that the dimension that they had reached didn't seem to have any violent life forms. They had found a couple of planets that would support their species. This is what had prompted me to ask. The commander had also asked if Lank and the other Cammeels wanted to go with them. Lank had told him no, they would stay with us no matter what happened. When I had asked to copy the dime warp device Lank was as happy as a dog with two tails. He urged the commander to agree. He still wasn't sure and said he would have to contact his leaders to get their permission. This meant he would have to use the dime warp to get to their new home. I asked him how long he would be before he came back with an answer. He said he didn't know. It was with mixed feelings that we watched the Camneel ship dime warp. We had arraigned a meeting point if the answer was yes, if it was no we wouldn't see them again. We could only wait. For weeks we travelled without any word. I think Lank felt the worse because they were his own people. We met the Xiobargs again. We knew they were still looking for us. Luckily for us it was only a small force, two dozen fighting ships and about thirty freighters. Barney was for capturing some of them and using them to create space among our crowded freighters. The only thing wrong with this idea was that we didn't have the facilities to fit any captured ship with weapons or more importantly the cloaking device, They would stick out like sore thumbs.

Another problem was wether to avoid them or wether to attack. With the look on everyones faces I decided to attack them. It might cheer everyone up, at least it would take their minds off of the problem of the Cammeels. We were just about to wade into them when the ship I had left at the rendezvous point with the Cammeels called us up. The Cammeel ship had just appeared and the commander wanted to talk with me at once. I was filled with hope as I said I was on my way. I was about to issue the order to make all speed to my ships when we picked up a signal. It was from the Xiobargs. The commander of the enemy ships must have picked us up on his scanners, I didn't realise we had got that close to them. He was demanding to know who we were and what we were doing in their space. I really didn't have time to mess about with him, but if I didn't answer, he would contact someone else and they might figure out who we were. I didn't know how long it would take to fit the dime warp devices, if the Canmeels had agreed to let us have them that is, and the last thing we needed was a battle with the Xiobargs. As the meeting point was over a weeks sailing away I decided to take a chance by wiping out the Xiobargs. This I reasoned would gain us the most time, if we ignored them they might try to follow us. I issued my orders and we attacked. The freighters were the first to go, they were easy meat.The cruisers were next and finally the six motherships. I hoped we had stopped any signals but to be on the safe side we left the battle site at full speed, our casualties were light. We had vastly outnumbered them so six or seven of our ships had simultaneously fired on an enemy ship. We reached the meeting point without further mishap. The Cammeel commander came aboard my ship and passed his leaders message. They wanted assurances that we wouldn't attack them, that we would share our knowledge with them and one or two minor details. I agreed to all of them and asked

Lank to return with the commander to reassure the Cammeel leaders of our good intentions. The Cammeel commander looked funnily at Lank when he said "Yes sir." I wondered how long we would have to wait this time for an answer. I was going to stay right where I was till I got one. I posted look outs and waited. We waited a month ,it was the longest month of my life, everything was quiet but nerves were stretched to their limit! It was uncanny to be watching the screens and suddenly out of nowhere a ship appeared.

A big ship at that! This must have been how the Xiobargs felt when one of our ships suddenly appeared in front of them! The news was good, we had permission to copy the Cammecl dime warp devices and as a show of good faith the Cammeels had brought enough materials to out fit every ship we had. The bad part was that it took us three months to do the job.

I had the freighters done first and as the first of them dime warped. I gave instructions for them to find suitable planets for us to start rebuilding our federation. When every ship had been fitted and they started to dime warp. I took a last look at our screens. This was my dimension and I promised that one day I would be back. My ship was the last to dime warp. When we arrived at our destination I was a little surprised. I expected it to be different but everything looked the same! The prof did try and explain it to me but I think he realised that he might as well talk to the ships bulk head. We found a couple of worlds that suited us down to the ground. We have a thriving community once again Our industries are up and running, we can feed ourselves and best of all, the Cammeels have joined our federation. I think that Lank was responsible for this. The Prof has been hard at work with his inventions, some of which are a positive liability. I sometimes wonder who's side he is on! He has come up with one good idea though. It is a matter transmit er He wants to use it for travel between our worlds, transporting goods and people in seconds, I thought of another use for it. Transporting bombs from our ships onto Xiobarg ships. At the moment though the Prof can only transport something about half a mile. This means we would be nose to nose with the enemy. We have plenty of time and I have all the time in the world.

The End.

Milton Keynes UK
Ingram Content Group UK Ltd.
UKHW020648120124
435917UK00016B/691

9 781917 007283